SHOE FET
A Woman's Love for Her Shoes and Her Men

SHARON BENNETT and
BEATRICE MOORE

COPYRIGHT @ 2002, Revision 2016
SHARON BENNETT
BEATRICE MOORE

EDITED BY: John DeSimone and Beatrice Moore

COVER ART BY: Sharon Bennett, & iStock Photos

Thank you God for allowing us to find & live our passions & purpose.

To all of our family and friends whom we hold dear. Thanks for all the love and support!

This is a work of fiction. Names, characters, places, and incidents, are a product of the author's imagination or used fictitiously, and any resemblance to actual persons, living or dead, events or locales is entirely coincidental.

For entertainment purposes and personal suave, you will need to know how to compare a shoe to a man. Like shoes, men exude many styles and personalities; and like shoes they do not all fit! Shoes also have no brains nor do most men, or so little they could fit it in the heel of a basic pump. I can only tell this story from my own experience that is from the females' window. However, these experiences are not unique and in fact plague both genders. Nothing in this world is perfect. No matter how hard one tries, there will be mistakes. Do not be so critical, accept it and move on. Enjoy this moment in life.

From what some of my male friends tell me, and I agree, there are pea brained inconsiderate women as well. Touché. Regardless of their imperfections, I am proud to know the male gender we call our brothers. In order to obscure the guilty, their names were changed.

SHOE: The basic dictionary will define "shoe" as an outer covering for the foot, usually made of leather, fabric, or plastic, with a stiff sole and usually not reaching above the ankle. Boots reach above the ankle.

MAN: An adult male human being with a particular occupation, responsibility, and background. Well, hopefully an occupation and a sense of responsibility. Without these main qualities, you are not a man. You are only a male.

INTRODUCTION

Shoe fetish is a casually written novella about three teenage girls, in south Texas, as they stumble from puberty to adulthood, trying to come to terms with their true feelings and desires. They acquired their knowledge of relationships through failed, abusive, and socially unacceptable affairs. The young women equate some of these relationships with styles of shoes. In the odyssey of the relationship maze; torment, strength, insanity, love, and even death were found. The girl's relationship with each other suffered years after college. They rekindled their friendship at a twenty-year high-school reunion. However, no one would have guessed the turn this road would quickly take.

This story is told through the eyes of its central character, Carmen Robertson. A regular southern teen. Some say Texans have a language all their own. These three Professional women endured some of life's greatest hardships during the spring of their lives.

CHAPTER 1

While flying high in the sky, I gazed out the window. The city was so beautiful at night. The lights glistened in their picturesquely geometrical patterns. They looked like toy houses and cars. The human race has advanced so far with its modern skyscrapers and homes. Men think they can do anything. God has been good to us; He is so mighty. What has taken years for man to build, can be destroyed in one cataclysmic event, like a tornado. I think about this type of thing frequently, because I could have been dead from a catastrophic event. Texas is part of tornado alley.

When asked, I tell people I had a good life. Even a charmed one. Life for me was not easy, especially when it came to affairs of the heart. God had blessed my life, but it came at a high emotional price. I could be happy one day and sad the next, melancholy, that is me. For as long as I can remember, I have been that way. It started in my teens. That is about the time I started feeling this strange irresistible attraction towards boys. What a coincidence!

It's June 1995, which marks a special weekend. I am heading home for a twenty-year high-school reunion in San Antonio, Texas. I hope to see a long lost friend. She and I were like sisters and we shared many good and bad times. Bethany Childs and I somehow lost touch a few years after college. She went to Prairie View A&M University, and I, Carmen Robertson, went to Sam Houston State University. It was a new life with new friends and the pressures of class work. It became extremely difficult to keep in touch, especially, when changing residences and phone numbers. Usually, we kept in touch through our parents who have had the same address and phone numbers since the middle seventies.

I am looking forward to this school reunion because I have missed her, my Buddy, my confidant. We have not talked for ten years, and life just has not been the same. I also want to see what everyone has been up to and show off my girlish figure.

I remember exactly how Bethany and I met. We were in the seventh grade. It was in our physical education class. I remember us running track and jumping hurdles, as well as complaining about it. She was such a friendly person with a trusting and positive attitude.

The pilot was announcing our approach to San Antonio. Land of the Spurs and the Alamo. The "*Fasten Your Seatbelt*" light blinked on and the flight attendant was collecting passengers' debris from the dinner meal, which was cold as usual. The most you could expect from these meals was gas. Served me right.

Next time, I should eat prior to going to the airport.

My sister, Liz, will be picking us up tonight from the airport. I missed her, her sons, and my parents. At least we talked on a regular basis. I bet my mother has one of her wonderful home cooked meals ready. She always makes such a fuss when the kids and I came home to visit. I have been a single mom for ten years and damn good at it, I might add. While working six years with a major insurance firm, I finally completed medical school. A long-awaited triumph in spite of some poor choices. I have also kept up with aerobics and weight lifting. Yes, a nice size eight, with cut arms and abs.

As I leaned over to wake my children, I made sure to fasten their seatbelts. I whispered, "Wow, I love them so much." What a blessing they have been to me, even if their father turned out to be shit. My divorce was hard. Sometimes, I wondered if I would ever fully recover. In addition, putting myself through school for a second degree was torturous. I would never trade these two kids for anything in the world.

Their father died shortly after our divorce was final. Some sort of accident involving alcohol and drugs. The police investigated the suspicious circumstances surrounding his death. They had a lot of nerve questioning me. The police arrested no one for the murder. The kids' upbringing fell upon me, and I am glad that I kept up the premiums on their father's life insurance policy, which would afford them a good college education, as well as a lower mortgage for me on a beautiful two-story brick home in an upscale neighborhood southwest of Atlanta. My parents are an excellent support system.

This reunion trip will also allow them time to visit with past school friends. My son, Jerrick, is 17 years old and a big-eyed, long-lash, dimpled cutie pie. My 15 year-old daughter Sharena is extremely smart, with a tiny frame, and such a beautiful softie. Sure, maybe I am a bit prejudicial when it comes to them. One thing I have never believed in was calling a child cute or beautiful, when they were butt ugly. All children are precious and a gift from God, but not all of them are cute.

Smooth landing. Yeah, that is the kind I like. As soon as the plane stopped at the gate, everyone hopped out of their seats and scrambled for their bags. What was the rush? Did they think the plane was going to take off before they could debark, or that their family would leave them if they did not get off in one minute? Rather than be crushed by all those bodies, some which may not be too fresh, we patiently waited until the plane was almost clear. The children and I anxiously strolled down the ramp to the waiting area and there was my big-eyed sister and her two cute boys. We hugged and kissed, walked arm-in-arm to the baggage claim. Her boys love my son. They think he is cool. They like to wrestle with him; or more like it, thrown around by him. They are ages five and seven now, and quite the chatterboxes. We loaded the car and headed for home.

"Well, Carmen, have you found a man yet?"

"Hell no, and I'm not looking for one either"

"Girl please, you mean to tell me that in two years you haven't found a man in Atlanta? That is a man Mecca. I know they have some fine honeys there?"

"True, there are some fine men in Atlanta. Black, White, Arabian, Jewish, Latino, and even French o-oh-la-la. Mastering my career as a Dermatologist has kept me busy. Besides, you cannot move too fast. I do not just let any man come around my children. For the most part if the men aren't gay, they are married, or think they are God's gift to women and you should be grateful for a date."

"What? You've got to be kidding."

"Don't get me wrong, now. I have nothing personal against gay people. It is not a lifestyle for me, and only God can judge, so I leave that up to Him."

"What about at church?"

"Liz, please. For one, I do not go to church to meet men, and two they are sometimes worse. You know, like an octopus. Please, you aren't dating either, so let's drop that subject for now, okay?"

"You're the boss."

"My goodness, San Antonio still has some bad ass drivers. They must get their licenses out of Cracker Jack boxes."

"Right, like they don't have bad drivers in Atlanta."

"Girl you said that right. What gets me is how some people try to be highway monitors. If I get a ticket, then the only one who is going to pay for it, is me. It's a sure sign that you're going too slow when a lot of people are passing you. So, just move your ass out of the way."

"I hear that, Carmen."

We spent the rest of the ride in silence, except for the rap music my kids wanted to listen to, and the chattering of my cute nephews. Just when my butt has had enough of sitting, we pull into my parents' driveway and it was as if I am a kid coming home from school again. Nothing has changed, from the manicured yard to neat and tidy inside. My parents have good taste, but they do not splurge. My father is a retired judge and my mother still does real estate part time.

They have nice furniture, but it is not a cluttered effect. The ample sized foyer wall is full of plates from the places they have traveled. The aroma of home cooking hits my nose almost as fast as my mom grabs me for a hug.

"How's my baby doing?"

"I'm fine Momma, but then you just spoke to me last night, so, I guess you know that. How are you and Daddy?"

"Fine Carmen, he's in there sleep, thinking he's still awake watching T.V. Go wake him up. By the way, your friend Bethany called. Said she couldn't remember the street we lived on and she'd been calling all the Robertson's in the phone book to track us down. Said to tell you she's coming to town for the reunion."

"Really Momma? My gosh, I was hoping to catch up with her. I'll call after I talk to Daddy."

"Kids, come here to Granny and give me my sugar."

I quietly approached Daddy, wondering if I should wake him or eat some of that tasty baked chicken I smelled. I am hungry and that plane food does not hold a candle to my Mommas' cooking. The eating will have to wait. Because, I was raised with manners. My father has a receding hairline that has been working its way back from the forehead to the middle of his head. I love to pick on him about it, by kissing him on his forehead or popping it with my finger. I decided to go with the kiss this time.

"Hi, Daddy. Do you know you're sleep and clutching the remote?"

"Hey, baby. Naw, I wasn't sleep. Just resting my eyes. You know?"

"Yeah, I know."

Just then the kids rushed him yelling, "Papa." After the preliminaries were over, we washed up for dinner. We all gathered at the table after helping mother prepare the plates. As our tradition, Daddy led the prayer and each person said a bible verse, and then dug into the food. We enjoyed seeing each other and did a little catching up as we ate. Liz suggested that we go shopping since the malls did not close until 9 p.m., and I did want to do some shopping for the reunion. You know I had to have the *perfect* outfit and the *perfect* shoes. She agreed to drive me after dinner.

WHEN I WAS YOUNG

Well, when I was a young one
Growing up long, tall, and thin
I would reminisce on
Mommas' guiding hand.
She walked, talked, and prayed with me
my soul would not be lost,
To her I owe it all, I can never pay the cost.
She is the gleam in my eyes,
and the light in my heart.
To you dear Lord I pray, please,
That we should never part!

Carmen

CHAPTER 2

"Hurry girls. Please stop that horsing around and finish your packing. I would like to get on the road to San Antonio before dark."

"Bethany, calm down. I'm driving, so, we'll be there before it's too late."

Bethany Childs lived in the suburbs of Dallas, Texas with her husband Chadwick "Chad" Parker, whom she married after a short courtship- defying both conventional wisdom and her better judgement. The marriage turned out to be the best decision she ever made resulting in three beautiful girls- Angela, Michael and Cooper who are ages 12, 6 and 4 respectively. As expected, the two youngest daughters engage in a severe case of sibling rivalry, badgering each other constantly, vying for attention from both Bethany and Chad. You really cannot blame them for seeking Bethany's attention. Bethany is juggling a demanding career as a wife, mother AND interior design consultant (which for most anyone else any combination of 2 out of the 3 career paths would be enough!) It does not stop there…she also owns an upscale boutique catering to a very exclusive clientele. As a result, she has clients around the world, most of which she met during her modeling days. She often travels to decorate their homes as well as offering them personal shopping experiences direct from the runways of Paris and Milan. Bethany has managed to merge and share her loves of fashion and home design by co-authoring two books on decorating and dressing with taste. As you can see, Bethany is more of a Renaissance girl. She kept her maiden name to maintain some personal identity and a level of freedom. Chad, her husband, is a successful commercial banker. Chad went to high school with us. He was a good basketball player and honor student who many thought would pursue a pro-ball career. He had the talent and the good looks to be anything he put his mind to! They reunited through a mutual friend when Chad needed his posh condominium redecorated. Bethany checked his financial resume before pouring on the charm. Some say it was love, some say love of money. Well, whichever the case may be, it was love nonetheless.

They had an extremely large and lavish wedding. Twelve bridesmaids and groomsmen, many who were either models, professional athletes, or bankers and all were extremely good looking. I was the maid of honor, and the best man was gorgeous. *It* (you know what *it* I mean) crossed my mind once, and left as quickly as it entered. Bethany and Chad share a six thousand square foot, two story, European styled home in a gated community. Regardless of Bethany's reason for marrying Chad, they are great together. Chad is a good man. He truly loves Bethany and they share a wonderful life. She loves him and their three girls reflect that love.

"Girls, girls, please stop bickering and get dressed so we can go."

"I don't know what to wear," whined Cooper.

"Why don't you girls wear the cute purple jumpers your grandparents sent?"

"We're not triplets, mom," sighed Angela.

"No, no. My button. I can't touch my button, if I wear the jumper," yelled Cooper.

"Mercy, child. You cannot handle a five-hour road trip without touching your belly button. Trust me; you will not die, if you cannot touch your button. One day it is going to fall off. I do not care what you wear. Just get dressed, so we can get out of here. Angela, help Cooper. Chad, are all the windows locked? Did we stop the newspaper delivery? Did we forward the calls to our cell phone?"

"Bethany, yes all of that has been done. Why you so keyed up? We've been back to San Antonio to spend time with the family before?"

"I know that. It hasn't been the twenty-year high-school reunion before. I'm excited about seeing Carmen. I finally spoke to her mother and she said Carmen is definitely coming."

"Oh yeah. You guys were really close buddies."

"Buddies! We were like sisters. Actually, better than sisters. In a family, you can't pick your siblings and you may not like them very well. We picked each other to share our deepest secrets. That's something that just doesn't go away with time. You know what I mean. I love her and I miss her."

"Yeah, baby. I understand."

"Great. Besides, you know I have plenty of shopping to do. I'd like to go to the mall tonight before they close."

Bethany and Chad herded the girls and the dog into the SUV to begin their 4-hour journey from Dallas to San Antonio. As the SUV rounded the circular drive and exited through the gates of their estate, Bethany mused to herself, "Well done, not bad from a little girl from SA." However, before they could get on Interstate 35 South, the first stop was the kennel. They had to check in J.B. (James Brown), their frisky black cocker spaniel. Bethany's mom just did not like the idea of a dog in the house and JB was definitely a spoiled pooch who could never survive the elements. Therefore, to keep JB safe and sound from Mrs. Childs and her trusty broom, the kennel was the best bet even if the girls were totally against leaving their 4-legged pal for the weekend. Besides, JB was excited to be at the kennel and with his four-legged playgroup for the long weekend.

The ride to San Antonio was over two hundred-fifty miles. The girls sat in the back listening to music, coloring, and chattering. Bethany and Chad engaged in small talk while she occasionally daydreamed of what the reunion would bring. Suddenly, Michael ranged out.

"She's touching me. Cooper is touching me."

"Cooper stop touching your sister."

"But, I like touching her, Mama."

"She's touching me again, Mama. She's touching me."

"Michael stop yelling. Cooper, please don't touch her again. You're stressing her out. Now stop it."

Angela rolled her eyes at the bickering of her younger sisters, and continued listening to her music.

The family arrived in the Child's well-maintained modest neighborhood where the homes averaged 1200 square feet and inhabited by many of the original homeowners from the early 1960's. Chad turned into the driveway after four and a half hours, and let out a deep sigh of relief. Being the only male in his household, he was happy to arrive so he and Mr. Childs could have some much needed male bonding time. Greeted warmly at the door by Bethany's parents and settled their luggage in the usual rooms. The girls then begged permission to run down the street to see their fraternal grandparents.

Mr. and Mrs. Childs were showing signs of aging and they had had medical problems through the years. Their small three-bedroom home was neat and well decorated in a mixture of Victorian styled couches with the plastic coverings; and eighteenth century styled dining room furniture with matching china cabinet. Bethany had tried for years to make over the house, but her mother would have nothing to do with what she considered as "that fancy modern style in those books of Bethany's"- Mrs. Childs liked her "stuff" just the way it was.

"Bethany, I was wondering if you could finally clean out that old closet of yours. Any clothes or shoes that you don't want, I'll send to Goodwill. Your father and I want to convert that room to an office with built-in bookcases in the closet."

"Sure, Mother. I can do that. I know you wanted me to do it for months and I appreciate you not taking it upon yourself to unload my property. That closet holds many memories for me. I'll take care of it tomorrow."

"Oh, by the way Bethany. Your old friend Carmen called."

"What? Why didn't you tell me sooner? I'll call her back right after I eat."

Bethany and Chad washed up, had a bite to eat and then went to check-in with his parents. Chad's older brother became an engineer and was now a state senator. The family is naturally extremely proud of him, which is evident in the many pictures and awards that cover the walls like wallpaper. Chad is the baby of the family, as is Bethany, and he will always be "Momma's youngest." It is funny how you never seem to grow up in your parents' eyes. You will always be a child, no matter how old you get. It seems every adult in the neighborhood looks at all of the young people as if time stood still.

The family spent time with chitchat over the next hour or so while the girls were in the Parkers' backyard playing. Bethany checked on them a few times to make sure there was no high drama between Michael and Cooper. Noticing how Bethany was hovering over the girls, Mrs. Parker assured her they would be just fine out back. Chad reminded her that they all played outside like that and lived to see another day. "Yes, you guys came out of this neighborhood and did alright for yourselves. So I am 100% sure that a little cut or scrape from Mother Nature won't kill those citified grands of mine," Mr. Parker chuckled. Bethany shook her head and realized she was being a bit overprotective and they were right. They settled in for a nice conversation and some catching up on the latest escapades of Senator Parker. Bethany glanced at the wall clock. She needed to call Carmen. She then bid her in-laws a good evening, hugged and kissed her girls, then kissed Chad firmly and promised him more of where that came from and took her leave.

As Bethany stepped out on the front porch and began her short walk home, she noticed how the sun was still blazing bright at seven-thirty in the evening thanks to the long summer days of south Texas. Adorned in her designer sunglasses, chino pants, navy t-shirt and espadrilles, she pulled her chestnut colored hair back into a ponytail with a scrunchy that she wore around her wrist. "I've got to catch up with Carmen," she said aloud, giddy with anticipation as though twenty years had not passed.

Bethany was always well dressed. Looking at her, you would know she modeled professionally. You know the type. Always dressed to the tee, no matter what. You could ring her doorbell at three a.m. and she would look like you interrupted her lingerie shoot. You would never see her in a store with rollers in her hair, or house shoes on. No, that would be too tacky for her taste. Actually, you would never catch me looking that way either.

She opened the front door of her parents' house and rang the doorbell as a safety measure. Known to be quick on the draw, if they suspected foul play, Bethany did not want to alarm them. They seemed to be getting more and more forgetful but that was to be expected.

"Hey mom and dad, it's me. I have to freshen-up. That drive and drama did me in," Bethany called out as she walked down the short hallway to her room. She dialed the Robertson's number but got a busy signal. "Hmm, they still haven't gotten call waiting. I am not surprised. Neither have my parents. Well, that does it. I bet Carmen is at the mall. I will just try my luck at North Park. I had my heart set on going there anyway to see my friend Noela who is a personal shopper at Saks." Carmen hung up the phone and began to sort through her garment bag for something to wear. She chose a crisp khaki tailored three quarter sleeved shirt, which buttoned down the front, with matching Capri slacks and brown leather mules. After hopping into their SUV, she adjusted the mirrors, checked her lipstick, and backed out of the drive, headed for the mall.

FRESH MEAT

Thinking, remembering a life does cry
Hoping to render an antique style
Void of indebted agile
Gathered, confronted with the sharp shears
Postured and crouched as it devours the years

Drinking her blood and love with its luscious taste
Why pilfer the life of a sweet miss, why waste
Bellowing your assertions of ill held reverence
From a deep dark place the beguiled head quickly reared
Because I love her, it sneered

Carmen

CHAPTER 3

Liz and I decided to go to the North Park Mall. It is the closest, and it has some nice stores. We have a great time, giggling, chatting, and talking about the strange looking people after they have walked by. We found several outfits and tried them on, but nothing that shouted, "Damn, she's fine." We saw absolutely, no good-looking men as we strolled around. The lack of datable men was one reason I left San Antonio. In addition, the party scene was about dead.

It's the same three clubs that open and close. So small that they look like roach motels for people. When you go to a club, you are on an eternal "pimp alert" with all the played out players still sporting aqua suede on leather stacked heels with blue slacks and coordinating shirts. Moreover, a player would not be a player without his brim. Oh yeah, that's definitely vintage seventy's Super Fly, Who loves ya baby, Dynamite, Get down jive, Dance Fever, Moving on up, Mackin, all come back to haunt in a big bad way! Damn, I see why some women just give up and become lesbians or find maintenance men.

It is not that I did not have any dates, I did. However, eventually something always went wrong. Either the men did not want to settle down, stating, he had liked to keep his options open; or they wanted to settle down but the sex was terrible; or my kids just did not like them. That was important to me that my children like him. If a man could not accept my children and take us all out from time to time, then he had no place in my life.

All right now, this is the dress. Right here in Dillard's formal wear section. A short bright red spandex job, that flares out a bit at the bottom, with double straps that extend from the bodice, around my neck, to the back. Yeah, time to try it on.

"Liz, where's the dressing room?"

"Over here Carmen. I'm going, too. Girl, you are going to knock them dead in that dress and you have the body and long legs for it, too."

"Oh, excuse me. I didn't mean to bump into you. I wasn't paying attention. Aaaaaahh, Oh my Lord, Bethany Childs! I don't believe it. Where have you been?"

"Carmen, it's a long story. But girl, I've missed you, too. I only came hoping I would run into you."

"Me too. Where are you staying?"

"At my parents' home. They still have my room the way I left it, clothes and all. You know I still have the letters you wrote me after you moved away during junior year in 1973."

"Really. Then I must confess. I still have the letters and cards you sent me."

"I see you've found a red dress? Go ahead, try it on."

"I will, but are you leaving?"

"Actually, I was heading to Saks, but no. I am staying here and not leaving until you try on that dress."

My God, Bethany looks the same. A beautiful young light skinned woman with big eyes and a big smile. She has always been taller. About five foot nine inches, not skinny, though. A well portioned young woman with big legs and breasts. I used to be jealous of her voluptuous figure, wishing mine were like that. I was a skinny girl, not malnourished, but thin. I hated the way my stockings bunched up around my ankles. If they stayed up at all, then I would have runs in them. I was a tomboy until my parents made me go to charm school during the summer before the seventh grade.

Wow, what a knock out. Yeah, this is the dress for me. After two babies, I finally get hips. It fits perfectly and shows every curve, with the length-stopping mid-thigh.

"Here I come ladies."

"Dang Carmen. Girl that is the dress for you," Liz said.

"Definitely, on the one. No one would guess you're a doctor. That dress makes you look like one of the beautiful people. Now we must go shopping for some shoes to go with it. Why don't you pick me up tomorrow morning around eleven and we will go to Saks? I have a friend who is a personal shopper and she knows where to find EVERYTHING!"

"Great Bethany, I'll see you tomorrow. I'll call when I'm on the way."

"Perfect Carmen, I love you and I'll see you tomorrow. Well, actually I'll see you later tonight. Aren't you going to the get acquainted party tonight?"

"Oh, I completely forgot about that! I was so excited to see you. Yes, yes. Of course I am. I'll see you there."

"Bye."

The mall was about to close. I grabbed a pair of sheer hose and some costume jewelry to go with my outfit. Moreover, the important part would be the shoes to complete the outfit. I was not looking for a man but I felt that this was going to be a special weekend for more reasons than one.

Being single affords you more flexibility. You can go around the house looking any way you want to. You handle your own finances and make all your own decisions. You depend on no one for love and emotional stability other than your family. In addition, if I wanted to go to bed without a shower or sex, than I could do that too. The single life had positive points. As Cameo would sing, "I'm living the single life." I owe no one any explanations for who I am and what I do. I did not actually graduate from Sam Houston High School because my family relocated during my junior year to St. Louis, Mo. In Missouri, there were only five Blacks in my graduating class and my brother and myself comprised two of them. However, the people at Sam Houston still claim me as their own and I like that.

Bethany and I did in fact see each other at the reunion get acquainted party. I remembered her husband from school. After greeting the other classmates, we sat with our heads together the rest of the evening trying to catch up. The party finally ended and we promised to see each other tomorrow morning.

We had no vast field of experience.
Our spirits connected, somehow, and
a partnership forged.
Together we would define and construct our
world
using each other for self-definition.

Carmen

CHAPTER 4

The night came and went so fast. I guess I was exhausted from the trip, because I slept like a rock. It was strange being back home in my old room this time. I felt as though I was in high school again. School spirit ribbons, buttons, and pom-poms on the wall. Old posters of my favorite groups. This was actually a newer, larger home that my family moved into after relocating from Missouri back to San Antonio after I went on to college. However, the furniture and décor was still the same, right down to my white turntable in a box with the colored polka dots.

The get acquainted party last night was nice. It was in the high school cafeteria, no decorations or anything. Nevertheless, no one seemed to mind. Everyone was cordial and seemed to be having a good time. Many looked like the years had been hard to them and many were on the memorial wall.

Lord, you never know. Here today and gone tomorrow. Life has at times been total chaos for me but at least I am here to live it. Thanks to Gods excellent grace. I had been saved from the pits of Hell. Just then, a light tap was on the door. "Come in."

"Good morning, girl. Are you ready to go get Bethany and go to the mall? Momma's preparing breakfast for us," Liz said.

"I'm ready, where are the kids?"

"Still sleeping, child. They were up half the night playing video games with my boys, and talking on the phone to their friends. See you at the breakfast table."

Momma had prepared a wonderful breakfast. I could hardly wait to finish my shower. That sweet cinnamon smell meant French toast, warm syrup, bacon, eggs, milk and juice.

My mother is such a sweetheart. We were closer now then we had ever been. I do not know where I would be without her. She is my number one best friend. Growing up she did not sit and explain sexual topics of life to me. I guess she figured if I did not know then nothing would happen. Maybe she just did not know how. She has always been in my corner.

Momma's best advice for fights was do not lose or you will have to deal with her when you got home. I was always getting detention or suspension from seventh through tenth grade for fighting. Though I was the tomboy type, I was attractive. Once I completed charm-school, it was worse.

I would plan my wardrobe out for three weeks, so that I would not wear the same outfit twice. Then I would draw out the hairstyles to wear with each outfit. Now I would dress like a Barbie doll but I would drop you where you stood, if you said the wrong thing to me. People were either jealous or they thought I was an easy mark. How wrong they were. I grew up fighting with my two brothers and their friends. I would not cat fight, but I could box.

Liz and I borrowed momma's Cadillac sedan Deville. We were going to need the room for the girls and our shopping bags. I planned on one pair of shoes, but I always came back with more, and Bethany was worse.

We stopped to pick up TheLetter DeLarue. Another friend from the old neighborhood, who was home visiting her family. She is two years older than Bethany and I. Also, extremely bright and with a heart of pure gold. She finished college in two and a half years, and went on through law school in two and a half years. Her family lived down the street from mine and she came down to introduce herself after we moved in, the summer of 1970. Her grandfather Mr. Archie DeLarue was born and breed in New Orleans, Louisiana. He loved that Cajun food and music. He lived a hard life and saved a lot of money. Money that he gave to TheLetter to get through college and law school. She was also one of three beneficiaries of his will. That gave her a total of $600,000.

TheLetter was a petite, dark brown-skinned girl with ebony hair just past her shoulders. The only thing I hated about shopping with her was that she could try on shoes right off the display, while Bethany and I had to wait for the sales person to bring our shoe size. That is not her fault, I guess. Her whole family is petite. Ten brothers and sisters in all. I guess that is why they named her "TheLetter". After ten kids, picking out names is not a task high on the list of things to do. The tallest person is her father, who is only five eight or five nine. He was a career Policeman and ran his family like a regiment. Not much touchy feely love went on there. Her mother is all of five foot two, and is one of the sweetest people this side of heaven.

TheLetter lives in Minnesota, in a nice brick custom two-story town home, with her only son. An adorable eight year old named Keon. Great place to party in the springtime, but a bit too cold for my taste in the winter. TheLetter had attended Harvard Law School, and currently employed as a junior partner for a major law firm. She and I have managed to stay in contact through the years and visit each other. Due more to her efforts than mine, since she is a lot better at it.

TheLetter was wearing a bronzed colored skirt set with matching sandals that tied around the ankle reminding me of the Roman sandals we wore in high school. I used to love wrapping those Roman sandal straps up around my legs. It gave them the illusion of being larger. However, the straps would always end up down around my ankles because my legs were so thin. Having children gave me curves, and my workout regimen gave my legs more shape. TheLetter was definitely stylish, but she somehow seemed tired and distant. I inquired if anything was wrong, but she denied it. She looked a bit pale, and had circles under her eyes. I had only seen her look that way twice before. Once when I visited her home, and the other time was prior to the birth of Keon. Since we disagreed so drastically on her choices of the opposite sex, she had stopped telling me everything that was going on in her personal life.

We arrived at Bethany's at eleven in the morning. Her mother invited us in and directed us back to Bethany's old bedroom. Now, Bethany's family is a bit different. Her mother, Mrs. Childs, twice divorced Bethany's father only to turn around and remarry him three times. The mother and father raised the three girls with drama. Naturally, this has always been an emotional issue for Bethany. One that she talks with few people.

Seated on the floor was Bethany at the door of her closet with a faraway look in her eyes. We all made ourselves comfortable sitting around her. Mrs. Childs returned with glasses of lemonade, chips, and dip on a tray. She smiled and sat the tray on a small table by the door. The parental relationship was not the best. Nevertheless, Mr. and Mrs. Childs have always been very nice, and Bethany and her sisters had shoes and clothes galore.

"Bethany, are you ready to go or are you cleaning out your closet?"

"Yes, you could say that. I guess I'm cleaning out my closet and some old baggage of my life, Carmen."

"Oh no! There she goes again talking in riddles. We were going to be here for hours, Carmen. I hate when she does that. You never know what she's really talking about."

"Shut up TheLetter and let her talk."

Liz, who is ten years our junior, began to laugh. "Boy, that's why I love hanging with you guys, there's never a dull moment."

Giving Liz a stern look, I turned back to Bethany. "Go ahead and finish what you were saying."

"Let me break it down for you. You see this shoe. It is a beautiful classic navy pump. A classy shoe that is always in style. Sometimes with a T-strap or as a comfortable sexy sling back. Every woman may have several pair in different colors. Why? Because it is her favorite most comfortable type shoe that goes with anything and in any weather. What is it each of us does when we have a date?"

"Shoot. I go out and buy a slamming outfit and a new pair of shoes," Liz spouted.

"Exactly! But the type of outfit and shoes you buy is based on your mood at the time, the type of guy you are going out with, and what you think would be attractive to him."

I had to admit Bethany was on to something. Gosh, she had a closet full of shoes and so did my sister Liz. I was not far behind. What about when we breakup with a man? We go shopping. Our closets become graveyards of failed relationships and the shoeboxes are like tombstones that serve as markers of the date, time, and "cost" of death! Yes, Lord, it gives the phrase "skeletons in the closet," a whole new meaning for sure.

Bethany continued to break it down for us in this basic manner. The pump, or T-strap, a popular styled shoe that has survived the changes of time. Sleek, sophisticated, great for a professional look. However, comfortable and allows room to play. The perfect shoe for the woman who has plans and aspirations for an ambitious and successful future. This shoe has stood the test of time, and has been in style for over a hundred years, in some form or another. That is a rare statement to make when relating it to a man.

A classic man would quite possibly be that Mr. Right. He would be intelligent, yet, have a sense of humor. He would know how to relax and hang loose when needed. However, he would have absolutely no problem handling his business and would do it with ease. We are not talking about a man who is stuck on himself or whose ass is so tight that he eludes constipation. He is built-well, physically; and takes pride in his health as well as his appearance. Clean shaven or a perfectly trimmed beard. His essence exudes the best cologne not the dime store knock offs. He cares for his car with regular maintenance rather than running it in the ground. He still realizes that his car is a machine and not his lover.

He is well organized and neat. Which, he reflects in his home. His priorities are straight and he knows that his possessions are just items and they do not define his being. His head is not too big to get through the door but his cut is not shaggy. One look at him and you know this man is confidant and a go-getter.

The classy man does not get jealous because he is sure of himself and of your love. He knows of your love for him and trusts you impeccably. There is no doubt and, therefore, no need to stress whether you will be there for him tomorrow. This man has been there for you and has loved and cared for you like no other. He does not want to make you hurt but make you happy. He is committed to a lasting and trusting relationship with only one woman and commits himself to finding all her secret treasures.

He wants to know what makes you tick, what is on your mind, and how you feel. He will not only listen intently, he will remember what you said. He does not mind discussion and knows the difference between talking and yelling. It is a lucky woman who finds a man like this and he will be lucky to find a classy woman.

Now, mind you two-dollar dimwits that do not know the difference between sexy and slutty, cannot expect to have a classy man. The most she can expect is to be is a notch on someone's bedpost as she thinks that someone is foolish enough to marry her after she has cocked her legs open for sex after the first night. Hoping he would want to take care of her for the rest of her life just because she gave him sex, and Guess what? He knows that if you gave it up easily to him then you have done the same to others. You are used goods. You cannot turn a streetwalker into a homemaker and this man's number is not 1-800-can-u-save-a-whore! She will likely get a buster. Good luck.

Bethany then reaches in the closet for an old brown penny loafer that has faded in some areas and run over to one side.

"Now, this shoe has got to go."

"Oh-oh-oh, I know. Let me do this one."

"All right, go ahead Liz." Bethany hands her the shoe.

"Wait. What is wrong with that shoe? It looks fine to me," states TheLetter.

"It would! Go ahead Liz," Beth said.

Liz begins to unravel her story for this shoe that was a cross between a drama and a horror film. An experience we have all had at least once. An old dull, boring penny loafer. The faded run over shoe. It is lived its life and gave you good service, but its day is over. The time for this shoe has passed. You know the type of shoe that leans way to one side because the leather or fabric of the shoe has worn deep to the side you favor; and what bit of heel the shoe used to have is no longer in existence. The color of the shoe has slowly and painfully worn off the back or the tip of the shoes, from scraping up against floors or concrete streets.

Well, guess what, the man that continues to wear that raggedy Jheri Curl, drip-drip, does not know that it is a played out style. It had its day! People with hard to control hair normally chose that style for the hope that it would look like naturally curly hair. You know the folk that want you to think it is good hair and that they had Indian in their family. When actually it is just thick and dry and they hoped that style would help it to grow to the length they had always dreamed.

This man thinks he is a player and God's gift to women. Watch out Ladies. This is the one you see coming from a mile away. It has happened to all of us at one time or another. Picture this scenario. You are at the club with your girls, enjoying the music, perhaps taking a rest break from dancing. As you look up you see the Jheri curl man coming. Drip-drip as he strolls in your direction, cheesing and grinning as he strokes his tongue across that gold tooth. He is wearing a loud colored patterned outfit and he struts like a peacock. Pimp alert at five o'clock.

"Hey baby, how are you doing? Wanna dance girl?"

Oh, my goodness, his breath stinks, too. "No, thank you. I just finished dancing and I'd like to rest for a few minutes," the poor damsel says.

"Well, girl I'll just sit here and keep you company for a while. Then we can dance."

You tell him that is not necessary and those seats belong to your friends. Then he stands behind you like a scarecrow, keeping all the other potential dates at bay. How dare he try to invade your space to monopolize your time; he did not pay your way into the club. You tried to let him down easy, but he is too dense to know it. What you need now Ladies is some dynamite. You are going to have to blow his ass out of there.

This type of camaraderie was grudging up too many old ghosts. Images that I really did not want to contemplate right now. Images that I had pushed deep down inside. In my family, we did get love and hugs, but there were stressors, also.

Being the daughter of an ambitious attorney and political figure was not all that it was cracked- up to be. The community looks up to your family and knows your father well. They do not know about the stress this public figure brings home, and it taken out on his family.

We all had our skeletons clanging in the closet, clanging their bones, and they would have to be cleaned out.

"So, what are you looking for in a man, Carmen?" TheLetter softly asked.

"I'm not looking. Nevertheless, the qualities that I would like in a man are for him to be smart, sensitive to my needs, and a good listener You know many men say they are listening, but will always do exactly what you said you do not like; or, will ask a question that you had been answered in your conversation to them. I also like a well-dressed man. Not necessarily designer clothes, but neat and coordinated. Let's see, a man that accepts me and my children as one, whose a hard worker, and believes in Jesus Christ as his Lord and Savior. Oh, and he does not have to be gorgeous, but it would be nice if he is a little easy on the eyes. Like I said, I am not looking. I'd just as soon kill a man, than deal with a bunch of crap that a relationship could bring."

"Is that all!" TheLetter spurns, "First, of all you wouldn't kill anyone. Secondly, girl you said a mouth full. You are too fussy. How can you find all those virtues in one man? I mean, is not that like impossible? You need to stop dating all those light skinned, greened-eyed, wavy haired brothers. They think that they are too cute, and every sister is running after them. True love can come in any package."

"No, she's not too picky, and there's no such thing as true love, Beth snarled. She just has higher standards than some folks we know.

If you have too low a standard, then you can get trash."

"You got that right, Bethany. Lord knows I have had my share of duds. TheLetter, it just so happens that these men approach me. I do not go looking for them. If they have a decent personality, then I will date them. Regardless of their eye color, complexion, or hair grade."

"Well, I prefer the dark-skinned brother, with the barely running car, and menial job. They are more appreciative," said TheLetter.

"Yeah, we know TheLetter DeLarue. You seem to like slumming in your trash and everybody else's."

"That's not true, Bethany. I don't slum."

"Well, it's either that or you're so dense that you fall for any rap line," I said.

"I heard that sistah. Carmen, remember when we were at the Aquarium nightclub one Saturday evening? This guy walks up to TheLetter, looking like he just crawled out of a dumpster and smelling the place all to be damn. He strolls up to TheLetter and says,

"Hey, sweet thang. If you got the dime, I have gotten the time. Where have you been all my life? Let's get married?"

"That's right, Bethany. I remember that. Then I said, "What page of the rap book did you get that from? You are so lame!"

"Correct, Carmen. Then TheLetter said, "I don't think it was lame, it was cute."

"Well, it was cute guys and I don't appreciate you two making fun of me"

"TheLetter darling, you are sweet and soft hearted, but girl you better toughen up or you'll be used for the rest of your life by men that don't deserve you," I said.

"Carmen's right, TheLetter. They have been telling you that since junior high school. Stop acting like some sick lost puppy who will take love from anything moving. Remember the old faded run over loafer," said Liz.

I could see that this was really hurting TheLetters feelings. For whatever reasons, she was feeling unloved and willing to accept it from anything in pants that looked her way and smiled. She fell in love quicker than anyone I have ever known. This manner of behavior often threatened to end our friendship. Bethany and I could not understand why TheLetter stayed so gullible. How could not, all the heartbreaks make her bitter?

"That's enough, Bethany! Leave her alone. It's her life and her choice in how she lives it," Liz interjected.

"Ladies, there is a party tonight," I said. "Let's go to the mall. This is bringing my mood down." Everyone agreed. "Liz, why don't you take the keys and you and TheLetter go ahead and get in the car."

Once Liz and TheLetter left the room, I had a quick chat with Bethany. "Bethany. I know TheLetter has always been more my friend than yours, but you are being rude and insensitive to her. I want it to stop, and I mean now."

"What, you're fighting her battles now, Carmen?"

"No, Beth. However, I feel like something is going on with her and your being mean and nasty won't help. So, cut the shit, okay?"

"All right. Hey, I am sorry but you need to watch your mouth in my mother's house. I guess I was taking my frustrations out on her. You know how I feel about women who choose to stay in abusive relationships. It won't happen again, Carmen unless she opens the door for more."

"OK; and my apologies for disrespecting the house. Let's get to that mall."

Once everyone was in the vehicle, we headed for the mall.

"Carmen, do you remember when we first met? My family had just located to San Antonio," Beth asked.

"Yeah, lucky us, Bethany. We had to ride the bus to Emerald, Jr. High School on the deep east side."

"Thank God, I didn't have to go there, Liz finally chimed in. There were some sure enough rough necks up in there."

"True, true, but not everyone that lived or went to school there were hoodlums. Don't be so quick to support the propaganda and stereotypes about what goes on at schools in neighborhoods that happen to not be middle class," Beth retorted.

We began to reminisce on our school days. Funny how reunions seem to make you rewind and fast-forward your life, as if it were a validation process of some sort. Saying, "You are who you are because of what you have been through; be it good, bad, or indifferent," I said.

FRIENDSHIPS LIGHT

When I find myself floundering in life's troubled waters
Constantly buffeted, by towering waves of uncertainty
or I'm caught within depressions swirling darkness
My spirit knows that you'll always be there for me

For during those moments when I'm unable….
To make it past the jagged reef of life's rocky times
I will head towards the lighthouse of friendship
Your steady beacon is always a welcome sign

So many times you've helped me through the darkness
Your friendship never failing to light the way for me
Yes, a friend such as you, is so very hard to find
So my light….you shall forever be

Carmen

CHAPTER 5

My first experiences with men were with my father and brothers. Though I loved them, I felt they were flawed. My father was spoiled by his mother and his wife; and he had trouble with the attention my mother poured on us, suspiciously, thinking we favored her over him. My brothers seemed weak and submissive, but I loved them dearly and was protective of them.

My squabbles with my brothers, Louie and Kennard, continued and I became a regular tomboy. I climbed trees, jumped off houses and fought boys. I even participated with the boy's Scout troop when my father became a Cub Scout leader. He wanted to raise his sons properly, but his daughter was learning the same lessons.

Louie was my older brother by one year and four months. He was the firstborn son and he thought he was special. Is there a prize for being first out the box or something? Which order of birth is the best one to fall in? Louie was always sweet and kind like a cuddly bear. He took after my mother. I, on the other hand, was more dominant and I soon took the position of leadership. This may not have been a good thing in the end.

Our parents worked hard to succeed in life and to ensure a better future for their children.

My father was heavily involved in legal civil rights issues. This was a double-edged sword. It was great for the community, but when he came home stressed, his wife and children suffered. He never laid a hand on his wife, but words could cut as deep as a knife and his were harsh and sharp.

We had a new neighbor. A single mother with two children, a son and a daughter. They were somewhat scraggly looking, but seemed nice enough. At least, until one unforgivable act. The girl, Kim, liked my younger brother Kennard. She would call me over to talk, knowing that my brother was usually with me. Kennard would talk to her brother, Jimmy; then, the boys would play.

One Saturday, we were in Kim's driveway talking. Kim's mother was sitting in the window of the converted garage, talking on the phone. The mother must have been talking to a man. Her speech was sexual and trashy. Kim then started trying to talk in the same manner to my brother Kennard. Kennard, of course, ignored her. He did not fancy girls, yet. Kim became angry and struck Kennard across the face with some thin wire she had. I was shocked. Kennard's immediate response was to strike back. Kim ran into the house crying to her mother. I took Kennard home.

Kim's mother came puffing across the street and demanded to speak with my father. This embarrassed my father. His son, hitting a girl. There was no discussion about what really happened. Our side of the story did not matter. My father wrapped a leather belt around his hand, pinned Kennard up in their small closet. Holding Kennard's pant leg tightly with one hand, he began wailing on one spot of Kennard's leg. He told Kennard he would break his leg. How dare he embarrass Daddy that way, and hit a girl? Mother, Louie, and I stood there traumatized. It was happening again. Liz began to cry in a corner. She was only two years old.

"Momma, make him stop. He's hurting him," I shouted.

My brother, Kennard, was screaming in a high-pitched squeal. "Okay, Daddy, okay."

"Stop!" I screamed, as I ran in, grabbed that belt and held on. I held on tight. I held on for my life. "I hate you. You are mean. You do not love us. Leave him alone."

I then took my brother in my arms and walked him to his bed. Kennard, once again, was punished for something out of his control. I really hated my father for that, and I still have not been able to get over it. How could he do community service to help others, but abuse his own. I know he did not see it that way; but that is exactly what it was. Tears were streaming down everyone's face, except for my father. My mother turned with disgust and went into the kitchen crying. An expression of self-realization emanated over my father's face, as he followed our mother. He had punished in anger, not love.

"Don't you ever touch my babies in that way; I will leave you, if I do not kill you first. Do you hear me, you bastard?" Momma said using a tone, I had heard neither before nor since.

"I'm sorry, honey. But, you can't just let them get away with stuff," he said.

"They're good kids and they don't get away with stuff. Just because your mother beat the shit out of her children when they did wrong, does not mean you can do that with ours. Do that again, I'll kill you," she said.

I had never heard momma curse before. Father then went and snatched his keys off the dresser and stormed through the front door and raced down the street in his car. Liz was still crouched in the corner. Grasping this, momma rushed back into the room to calm her.

One Saturday morning, in 1969, my brothers and I walked up to the neighborhood Junior High School in Corpus Christi, Texas. We had climbed the large trees over to the branches that leaned against the school. From the schools roof we could peer down at the couples that were in the doorways kissing and doing other things that looked gross. This one girl named Lucia was very pretty but our classmates called her nasty. She had a boyfriend by the name of Ricardo. The two of them were a good-looking couple, but they were always at the school on weekends, in the doorways, doing gross things.

My brothers and I watched. Then as they started home across the schoolyard, they stopped and Ricardo picked Lucia up to carry her across the yard. There were many sticker bugs, but why did she not just put her shoes on? When he picked her up, his left arm was around her back, but the right arm went up between her legs instead of under them. That ended our days of going up to the school.

However, that following Monday the whole sixth grade class met in the cafeteria for a film on hygiene, menstruation, and puberty. Darn if Ricardo and Lucia were not at it again. Did they honestly believe that because the lights were off, that no one saw them? Ricardo was sitting behind her and had his hand reaching under her dress. If a boy ever tried that with me, I would cut his hand off. I made it a point to avoid them.

Our family relocated from Corpus Christi to San Antonio, Texas the summer of 1970. My parents had enough. After several fights and school suspensions, they sent me through charm school at the community center. They had their fill of my tomboy ways and wanted to force me into the dwindling respectability of a Lady, a more presentable image for the daughter of a public figure.

Twice a week, for eight weeks, I learned to walk with a book on my head, how to sip tea, cross my legs, and put on make-up. I already had a natural knack for fashion and color. That I got from my parents, but some of the girls needed help in all those areas. The way some of those girls looked, I did not think make up was going to help. There were people that no amount of make up or wardrobe could help. They were just pure ugly. Life's experiences have since taught me, that a person's heart is more important.

Then I could not help but to wonder why two ugly people got together and then had the audacity to have a baby. Imagine your only gene pool being the ugly pool. Folk had a hard enough time getting through life without being ugly, too. The best part of class was when we had a fire drill and had to take the fire slide out the window. School was to start in just six short weeks, and I would be ready with my new image.

Time passed quickly and the first day of school arrived. The car ride was quiet. We had just dropped my younger brother off at Cameron Elementary. Now, Momma was taking Louie and I to Emerald Jr. High. I did not understand why Cameron was just three blocks away, but Emerald was about ten miles. At least it seemed far. I understood even less when I saw the school. A million thoughts meandered through my mind. Right in the heart of the lower income area and run down. I hated this. Having to make new friends was becoming such a hardship. We moved every two to four years due to my father's career ambitions. He was now an assistant district attorney. He had struggled many years in the south as an independent lawyer striving for equal rights for Blacks, and other minorities.

Momma completed the registration forms for school and kissed us goodbye. I wanted to scream, do not leave us momma, do not leave us. I fought back the tears because I did not want to appear weak, especially here. I was also worried about my brother, Louie. He was a year older, but we are in the same grade. He was such a softie.

Louie had to repeat sixth grade, while in Corpus Christi. It was the end of the school year, and we had gotten our grades. We always walked to and from school, since it was only two blocks from home. Kennard, then in third grade, received passing marks. I passed to the sixth with excellence.

Louie came running toward us. He was so excited. I asked him how he did. He shouted with such delight.

"I've been retained, I've been retained. I am going to seventh grade."

I tried to stop him and tell him what it meant, but Kennard and I could not catch him. He was too fast that day. Thank God, momma did not have the heart to whip him. He was broken hearted enough when she explained what "being retained" meant.

I have always felt, from an early age, that I had to protect my brothers. Once when Louie was in third grade, I was in second, and Kennard was in half-day kindergarten, we had a high school babysitter. The Elementary school was right across the street from our home in Corpus. The high school was just a few blocks away. High school let out forty-five minutes earlier, and the sitter was at the house when we arrived. It was a late fall day and Kennard was not feeling well. He had always suffered from one ailment or another ever since an aspirin poisoning where he almost died, thanks to me sharing what I thought was candy.

On this particular day Kennard could not get home quick enough before his diarrhea kicked in. Instead of being compassionate, the sitter got three switches from the backyard tree, locked Louie and I out of the house, and whipped Kennard until each switch broke. His screams broke my heart. Finally, she let Louie and I back into the house and promised the same fate would befall us, if we told our mother. I felt helpless and responsible. That is the first time that I wanted to kill someone. Why could I not help my brother?

When my mother arrived, we all got in the car to take the sitter home. Once the sitter got out of the car, I told my mother what had happened. Momma almost broke her neck trying to catch that girl before she got inside. My mother told the girl's parents that if she saw her again she would give that girl the same judgment that she handed down to her baby son.

The first bell for class rang, snapping me from my daydream. "I'll meet you right here after school. Okay Louie?"

"Okay, sis. Have fun and I'll see ya later."

I went through most of the day in a fog. The guys gawked at me and the girls rolled their eyes. Tomorrow we start riding the bus to and from school, great, that should be even more of a thrill. At least, they were city buses and not those ugly yellow ones.

The last class was physical education. This class would have been cool, except for one thing. We had to take showers afterwards, and those shower stalls looked like they could grow legs and walk. In addition, there was no privacy in the changing areas.

The girls sat on one end of the gym bleachers and the boys on the other. There were several scrag-a-muffin types here and there, sprinkled among the more studious types and others who were just on the edge of normal and who knew what. Then, a voice came out of nowhere.

"Hi, are you new here?"

"Yes, I am."

"My name is Bethany Childs. It is my first day, as well. You looked a little antisocial, so, I thought I would come over. Do you want to sit together?"

"That will be fine. I am Carmen Robertson. So, tell me Bethany, what made you so sure you could approach me?"

"Because, Carmen you are well dressed, your hair isn't all over your head, and you don't look like the rest of these rats. I figured what have I got to lose."

"You could have lost a tooth if I had whacked you."

"Oh, you got jokes. Yeah, I guess. Then it would have been on in here."

"Hmmm. Let's take a seat."

"Well, all right."

The instructor came in and blew her whistle. She was an average height, skinny lady whose knees were larger than the circumference of her calves. She also wore a poor quality short wig.

"My name is Ms. Thompkins. I will be your P.E. instructor. You will do exactly as I say and when I say. Do that, we will have no problems and you will pass this class. You can get your uniforms at Sears. The color is green. You will need white socks, a T-shirt, and a pair of shorts. Everyone is expected to dress out daily, starting tomorrow."

Let me see if I have this straight. We dress out daily, but we are to get one pair of shorts, socks, and a T-shirt. I am no math whiz, but it seems to me that we will need more than one outfit or this place will smell like a swamp. Oh, and do not forget a pair of thong sandals for those living shower stalls.

That is a hard arrangement for someone like me that does not wear the same outfit within a three-week period. That is why I learned how to sew. Since my family was not rich, sewing was more economical.

Bethany and I exchanged phone numbers and we chatted all the time. School was so much easier with a partner in crime. If we were not on the phone, we were riding our bikes, playing tetherball at recess, or in physical education.

There was this one chunky girl in our P.E. class, Extel. She must have been a size forty-D up top. On this particular day we were doing simple gymnastic routines. First, we were to tuck and roll on the matt, then walk the balance beam, do a cartwheel, and come around to jump over the horse. Things went fairly well, until Extel came up. She did all right until she jumped the horse and fell on her chest. Man, she rocked back and forth on her boobies, like a rocking chair. I had never seen anything like that. Bethany and I laughed, at first, but remembered our manners and went to help her up. She was sore the next day.

SAVE ME

Once held tight and secure
Kept from harm and danger
Love cherished and protected
Caught, if you might fall
Tears wiped when you cry
Never alone you thought
Who knew the pitfalls that you might endure
Far from that place you thought secure
Hold on tight and don't let go
For of God's precious hand you know
He'll wipe your tears from your face
He'll pick you up when you fall
Just cry out his name from the cold dark night
And believe that he will save me

Carmen

WHAT YOU SEE IS WHAT YOU GET!

CHAPTER 6

During my father's climb up the career ladder, he gained a close friend by the name of Mr. Harvey. Mr. Harvey and his family had relocated back to San Antonio before we did. Dornaye was one of his daughters. We were the same age and knew each other in Corpus Christi. She was also attending Emerald. We made plans to spend the night and catch up.

It was the spring of 1971, and I was to ride the bus home with her one Friday, after school, to spend the night. Dornaye was good people and all. I had known her longer than I had known Bethany and TheLetter, but our bond was not as close. However, it was nice to spend the night away from the house. That way I could avoid some of the stress of trying to measure up for my father.

My older brother Louie has always been quiet and to himself. He loved to sketch, draw, or paint spaceships and model airplanes. He aspired to fly. However, my father harshly admonished him about such fantasies. Louie went to see a psychiatrist, which was the first negative strike to make him feel stupid, mentally ill, and like a freak. He always worried about what other people thought of him.

The last bell rang and I ran to meet Dornaye at her assigned bus. Her family had a nice home on the eastside. It was about three to five miles from the school and one street over from the Village project apartments. I used to wonder who surveyed, planned, and developed that area.

We were riding along smoothly and chatting as young girls usually do. We sat in the first seat that faced forward, right behind the driver. Suddenly, I felt a thump on the back of my head. I placed my hand on the back of my head and reached down to the floor in front of me to pick up the object. It was a wad of paper. I turned to look at the knuckleheads in the back who became quiet and looked as if they were posing for a portrait.

"Paper fight," I shouted. Grabbing and balling up paper from my notebook as fast as I could. Dornaye joined in. By the time, we arrived at the stop the bus's floor was so full of paper that it looked like snow.

Several of the guys stood around waiting until Dornaye and I debarked the bus. This large mixed ethnic guy approached me, followed by an even cuter average height guy.

"Hey girl, you're pretty good at throwing paper balls," the large fellow said. "What's your name?"

"Carmen, Carmen K. Robertson."

"Cool, Carmen K. Your nickname is C.C. How about that?"

"I like it. C.C. it is."

"Good. My name is Buffalo Bellazario. Anybody tries to mess with you, just let us know. Any problem of yours is a problem of ours. This is my younger brother, Franco. That short yellow guy is Smitty. Over there is tall Melvin, that dark skinned brother is Leon, and the dude with the stutter is Paris."

"So, you're a friend of Dornaye's, huh? I've noticed you at school."

"Yes, Franco, she is and we have to go now." Dornaye slipped her arm into mine and we headed for the house, yelling, bye.

"Okay, but one more thing. There is a party this Saturday night at P.J's. If you can come on by?"

"Sure, I'd love to. See you then," I cooed.

"Yeah, yeah, school, school, party, party. We have to go Franco. See you guys later. Carmen, you think you're so cute."

"No. You think I am cute. Where the hell did that come from?"

"Nowhere, never mind. Let's just go home," said Dornaye.

We quickly took our showers and dressed for bed. We wanted to have that out of the way in case we fell asleep. We popped popcorn, drank Kool- aid, ate sandwiches, and candy. All while playing cards and calling boys.

"So, Dornaye, spill it. What's the story on that cutie Franco?"

"He and his brother Buffalo live in the projects back there. Their mother is black and their father is Spanish. He has a girlfriend and her name is Chastity, of which she has little," Dornaye smirked.

"Chastity. You mean that tall skinny stick from school?"

"Yes, and he has experience."

"What do you mean experience?"

"You know, Carmen. The nasty, bumping, sex, humping, screwing."

"I get the picture Dornaye. But, how in the world do you know that?"

"Everybody knows, Carmen. The girls been in love and cocking her legs open to prove it, and she wants everybody to know that's her man."

"Well, we'll just see about that. Let's call Bethany and TheLetter to tell them about the party."

The night came and went. Momma picked me up around ten that morning. She said it was okay for me to go to the party. Daddy would take all of us, if TheLetter's father would pick us up. Bethany, TheLetter, and I rode together, while Dornaye met us there.

The party was in P.J.'s back yard. There were colorful balloons hung everywhere. The stereo system and D.J. were set up on the covered patio, while the mingling and dancing went on in the yard. There was a decorated detached garage, too, with a black light to boot. There were two large barrels filled with ice and sodas, and there was a table full of food on the patio with the D.J.

Franco and I danced, but there were other cuties there and they were one to three years older. The girls and I were dancing fools. The music was great. Songs both old and new like, "Stop the Love You Save," by the Jackson's, "Natural High," by Bloodstone, "My Girl" and "Just my Imagination" by the Temptations, and you can't forget James Brown. You were not partying unless you went home with your feet hurting.

Chastity eventually showed up and hung on Franco like a cheap suit. The girls and I were chilling in the garage, drinking sodas and talking to Buffalo, Paris, Smitty, and Leon. Several couples were dancing to the *Funky Chicken*, *Shotgun*, and *Grazing in the Grass*. Suddenly, Paris started stuttering, "I-I-I l-i-i-i-k-e y-o-u-u-u." As he grabbed and started kissing me.

Man was he strong. The guys were pulling on him and the girls were pulling on me. After the fellas explained to him that he could not do that, Paris apologized.

Micah, my neighbor was there and came over to see if I was all right. Mr. Fine himself, ouch. This boy looked so good, it hurt and he was so cool. Especially, when he wore that black brimmed hat and his silver bangle bracelet. He played the saxophone in the school band at Sam Houston High School. He also played in a small local band called "Blue Hue." Micah was two years older, and he had some younger siblings. The band would often practice in our neighborhood and some of the kids would hang around to listen. Girls chased after these guys like crazy. Micah was always nice to me, but I was not initially attracted to him.

"Carmen, what's going on in here? Are you all right?"

"Yes, I'm fine, now. It was just a misunderstanding. Buffalo and The guys have handled things."

"I see. Well, do you and the girls need a ride home?"

"No, TheLetter's father is coming to get us," Bethany swooned.

"Okay, then. I'll see you tomorrow, Carmen."

Everyone waived bye to Micah. By seeing me tomorrow, he meant in the neighborhood.

On Sunday afternoons, the Guys got together and would play touch football in the street, in the fall. During the summer, it is baseball or basketball. It was so much fun. Someone would bring a radio for the music and the girls would cheer and dance. The best part was when these Guys got so hot that they took their shirts off. Oh-baby, Oh-baby-oh, they were so well developed.

Sunday afternoons were such a big deal that even guys from the next two neighborhoods would come over. Many of these fellas actually played on the school football, basketball, and track teams. Even the beautiful people came and actually sat on the curb to watch the games. These are the people acting as if everyone should be watching them. They are spoiled by their possessions and oblivious to the world's real issues. To them no one is better looking.

One Sunday, March 1971, I wanted to wear my new lavender pant set. Micah and I had been talking on a daily basis. For some reason I started to like him. There were all these strange feelings coursing through my body. I did not really understand it all because I had never liked a boy enough to care about what I was wearing.

Momma and Daddy would never have a heart-to-heart with me about sex. Their conversation encompassed one basic premise. Just do not do it! The best thing my parents could have done to protect me, would have been to sit me down and tell me about the feelings I might have when caring for someone. Tell me what to do in certain situations. Tell me I can always talk to them without the fear of ridicule or repercussions.

On this particular Sunday, I was leaving the house to go down the street and hang out with TheLetter before the football game. I was wearing a lilac pant set. The fabric was a stretchy polyester. The top laced up the front and the slacks were bellbottoms. I loved that combination because it made me look shapely.

So much so, that as I was exiting the door my Mom said, "Have you been having sex?"

I said, "no, why?"

"Because your butt looks bigger and when young girls are having sex their butt gets bigger."

What in the hell was she talking about? I never heard that and besides I had not even had sex. I am not even sure I would know when it happened. That comment probably came from the same educational repertoire as the old wives tale not to wash your hair during your menstrual cycle. Anyway, I decided just to leave it at that and go on to TheLetter's.

It was a great weekend and I had a lot of fun, even if my curfew for parties was ten thirty. The streetlights had not even been on long. It took me two years to get a curfew of midnight. Everyone knows the party does not get started until eleven.

The school paper came out later that week and Franco had dedicated a song to me, "You're a Big Girl Now, No More Daddy's Little Girl." What in the heck was that about? This boy has a reputation. However, you are not getting these goods, baby.

WHY MUST IT BE SO HARD?

WHY ALL THE DRAMA?

CHAPTER 7

Community sports were a part of every neighborhood and ours was no different. It was the summer of 1972, after our freshman year, and I had joined a citywide volleyball team, made up mostly of girls from the neighborhood. This was my first time signing up for an organized sport. Mr. Gray was our coach. He worked as an umpire and referee for a living. He had a set of fraternal twins that played on the team, as well.

The girls practiced hard and our team kicked butt. I liked the game so well that I tried out for the school junior varsity volleyball team my sophomore year. Bethany and I made the team. We practiced hard and when we were not at school, we practiced at my house on a net my father purchased. Now, I had three loves. When I was not playing volleyball with Bethany, I was dancing in a school or local talent show, and Friday nights was roller-skating.

On skate nights, we wore blue jeans with a brightly colored bandana tied around the leg. We always had routines worked out and would often skate in a line with the Guys. Yes, we were sharp. Skating both backwards and forwards.

Life was good and we had many friends. Many were the school's football and basketball players. Though Bethany and I were attractive, we did not date these Guys. We simply were friends. As far as we were concerned these Guys had too many females, many were our friends, chasing them; and, it was not the kind of self-absorbed scene we were interesting to us.

This year the fights and suspensions were almost nonexistent. People knew who we were and respected us. Bethany and I had been on student council in junior high and our freshman year in high school. We also played spades in the school cafeteria before first bell. We were a mean team of card players. We often played cards at home, mostly gin rummy. Bethany was good at cards.

There was no doubt about it we were tight partners in crime. We shared everything, including the revelation of our first. My first date was with my father. He took my siblings and me out to dinner. He instructed me that a real Gentleman would come to the front door to pick his date up, meet her parents, always open the car door for her, and pull out his date's chair. That Gentleman would also never lay a hand on me in an abusive manner.

"Don't worry Daddy. If he does, I'll beat him up," I would say.

My father would tell me not to let the boy touch me, especially for sex. In our household, the sex education was, "You don't ask questions."

My first boyfriend was Ray Washington. First grade in Corpus Christi. He was a skinny dark black kid that came by the house to visit after school. We knew his family from church, and they lived in our neighborhood. Sometimes during recess, we would play church. Ray was the preacher and our friends were the choir and congregation. We would holler, dance, and faint. Just like the church Ladies. One day Ray gave me a ring. He got it out of a Cracker Jacks box. It was cheap, but sweet because he said the red stone represented the love in his red heart. Ray and I never kissed nor hugged and that was fine with me.

Bethany and my first exploration anywhere near sexuality came in the form of our attraction to our ninth grade substitute science teacher, Mr. Dick Delgado. Oh, what an adorable Latino male. Rumor had it that this man's private part hung down to his knees.

High school is such a trip. Kids can be so silly and so gullible. Stories are over exaggerated and rumors fly. There was even a story told about a substitute science teacher; and, it was with this fantasy told about our substitute science teacher. None of the girls were late to class. Mind you, many of us girls had never actually seen any man's private parts and probably would not know one if it slapped us in the face! We spent the whole period staring at the man's crotch, hoping to get a glimpse of this infamous part of his anatomy. Of course, we never noticed anything, but spent the time after class clamoring that we had.

Sex was a weapon we did not know how to use and certainly did not understand. We snuck around; because, it seemed to be a mystery that our parents did not solve for us. We had to investigate. Since neither of us knew what we were doing and it was not this miraculous, wonderful experience, it did not deserve the title of lovemaking.

One night in the fall of our sophomore year, Bethany spent the night with me. My family had since moved from the three bedroom, one bath, one car garage, half brick home over to a four bedroom, two bath, two living areas, two car garage, full brick, covered patio home. We even had a second telephone line. However, I often drove to the old neighborhood to visit TheLetter and Micah.

We stayed up late watching television and eating popcorn. Once we were sure everyone was sleep, our serious girl talk began.

"Well, Carmen?"

"Well, what?"

"What was it like?"
"What was what like, Bethany?"
"Don't play stupid. The sex."
"Oh, that!"
"Yeah, that."
"It wasn't like people say. It happened fast, like I told you on the phone. He kissed me, hugged me, then he slowly removed my clothes while kissing me on my neck."
"Oh, my God, girl. Where were you?"
"Bethany, do you want to hear this or not?"
"I'm sorry, go ahead."
"It was at his house. We were sitting on the porch talking as we often did. His family was not home. They were out visiting a relative or something. We had been friends for a year now, talking about any and every subject. He had shared his hopes and dreams with me. He took me to his junior prom last year. He had even talked to me about the different girls he's dated and their ambitions."

He looked into my eyes and said, "You're the prettiest and easiest girl to talk to. I have never had a girl who was really a friend like you. I love you, Carmen."

"Feelings welled up in me like never before. I felt tingly all over. He took me by the hand and gently guided me into his house, into his bedroom. After, softly and slowly removing my pants, he laid me back onto the bed and climbed on top of me. I could feel this thick hard warm manhood between my legs. I was not sure what to do, so Micah was on his own. He put his hand down there and fumbled around a bit until he was able to find my passions opening. It took him a couple of minutes to get himself all the way in. Things were a bit tight and it hurt a little. Suddenly he retracted and there was this cold wet stuff between my thighs."

"Yuck, Carmen!"

"I thought to myself gross. Is this it? Then he got up."

"My girl," he said.

"As he tried to kiss me again, I quickly pulled up my pants and ran home. He tried to catch me, but couldn't with his pants still down around his ankles."

"Why did you run out?"

"I'm not sure. I was ill prepared for such a relationship, and though I liked the feelings I had before he touched me, I felt confused. Once he laid on me, things changed."

"Changed how, Carmen?"

"I don't know. It was like I am more vulnerable and embarrassed. Anyhow, I have been avoiding him all week and not taking his calls. At least until last night when I came home from practice. He was sitting on the front porch. Looking as handsome and cool as ever. His lips were full and soft. I could not help but to watch, as they danced when the words flowed out of his mouth. He told me that he really did love me and wanted to be with me, but if I wanted him to back off, then he would. To back off was indeed my desire."

I was not ready. What was it about, relationships? Was it that I did not fathom its depth? Sharing that first and unique experience with someone I viewed as a friend only complicated things. Besides, I thought it would be more romantic. Maybe with flowers or chocolates. This was someone I went to prom with, to dinner, watched the stars, and risked coming home past my curfew for.

My curfew was one a.m. for that special occasion, Micah's junior prom. However, not wanting to look like such a square at the party, I stayed an extra thirty minutes. My reward for disobedience was a strong slap across the face from my father.

"I have something to tell you, Carmen."

"What, Bethany?"

"Yesterday, I went to the five o'clock show with Greg. Well, that is what we told my parents. We actually went to his house to have sex."

"What? You little slut. You two have only been going together a few weeks."

"I know. But, I love him or I think I do, and we couldn't wait any longer."

"Love! What is that really? I mean I have known Micah for over a year and I cannot say those words. Not like that anyway. Maybe something is wrong with me?"

"Nothing's wrong with you, Carmen. Maybe you cannot say those words, but at least get better at how and when you have sex. Girl, you were in his parents' home. Next time, wait until a man can afford to pay for a decent place, a hotel. For prom, you knew your daddy was going to be waiting for you. You came home late and got the taste slapped out of your mouth. You know Mr. Robertson don't play."

"Yeah, I know. Hey, I feel like shopping. Let's go to the mall in the morning."

"Okay. Are you looking for anything in particular?"

"I don't know. A pair of flats or maybe some tennis shoes."

"Flats or tennis shoes mean that you're depressed and you don't care what someone else thinks. You just want to be comfortable."

"What are you? Some sort of shoe guru, Bethany? You know you have a shoe fetish, don't you? Maybe I should pay you a dollar for this good advice. You want a dollar Bethany? Goodnight girl!"

"Fine. I am just trying to help you out. Goodnight."

**GIRLS WILL BE GIRLS
AND
BOYS WILL BE BOYS
AND
THE MYSTERY OF LIFE STILL
REMAINS**

CHAPTER 8

It was the fall of 1973, my junior year in high school. Little did I know that another emotional upset was on the horizon? Bethany and I had worked hard and were chosen to be on A-string for volleyball. We were so happy to see our names on that list after tryouts.

The guys came and went. From the juvenile pranks and insensibilities to the dull and charmless pickup lines at the parties and clubs. There was Robert, who idolized Jimi Hendrix. He played his music and dressed like him. From the headband to the suede or leather vests with fringe, to the moccasin boots. He also wore these thick round glasses like Mr. Lippit. You know that Don Knotts movie when he turned into a fish. Maybe that is what attracted me to him. We dated about eight months in my sophomore year. However, we were never intimate and I did not love him. He was a senior planning to enter the army after graduation. He would be out of my hair then.

Next was Daniel. He was on the track and football teams. Doing so well that it earned him a scholarship. A sweetheart of a young man with manners. However, his kisses were like sucking on oil, yuck. It seems that if you care about doing something, you would want to do your best, even if it means extra practice.

Maybe no one had the heart to tell him. Lord knows, I did not.

It was October 1973, a Monday, when my father came home early and called a family meeting. As if, our opinion really mattered. He was offered a great opportunity for advancement, but it meant moving. It always did. He pointed out all the pros and cons and wanted our input. At least that is what he said, but we all knew to agree because that was what he wanted. We had only been back in San Antonio for two years, now he wanted us to move to Missouri. But, we dared not object to him. Because he was ripping us away from family and friends, he threw us a going away party to ease the pain.

The party was great and everyone I knew came, as well as, some I did not know. It was great fun. When it was over, I turned the lights off and I cried myself to sleep. The only good thing I could come up with for moving out-of-state was that it would be easier to break up with Daniel. This would be the fourth move and it was extremely difficult for me and my brothers and sister to adjust.

We packed our belongings and a moving company came in to handle the rest. The transition to our new home had to be fast and intense. My parents did not want us to be out of school for more than a week. Momma was a miracle worker. Her care for our family was priceless. However, Missouri soon became the state of Misery, for me.

MY SPIRIT

My spirit and soul often threatened to blow
Here and fro, when no knowledge of the
Destination did glow.

Through you God has blessed me with a
Tenderly heard and gilded smile
Oh, how I love you.
I'm sure you've known all the while.

Did my life begin the day I was born;
Or does it begin today?
What will I be to you or to myself?
What is my path and to what end will it
follow?

Carmen

CHAPTER 9

The winters in St. Louis were cold and harsh, which I could not become accustomed. To make matters worse Hazelwood High School had to run in two shifts in order to accommodate everyone. Unfortunately, the Robertson children had the six a.m. to twelve-thirty shift. I hated this with a passion because I was not a morning person. As far as, I was concerned it was still nighttime. Who in the hell wants to get up at four- thirty in the morning in order to be dressed and ready to catch the bus to school. It is early, cold, and the classes were boring. My God, what matter of hell is this? Save me, save me now.

Life thus far was dealing me some messed up cards. Yet, I still could not fathom the lurid hand that was to unfold. It was as if the grim ripper had been lurking in the dark shadows waiting to steal my innocence.

We lived in a racially mixed middle-class neighborhood. The people were nice and we made friends quickly. Friends of the same race. Surprisingly, I experienced more racism in this northern state then I ever had in Texas. History books tell us that Missouri annexed into the United States as a slave state in 1821, as part of the Missouri Compromise. It was settled (as a territory) mainly by whites who were slaveholders. At one point, when seeking statehood, they wanted to ban free blacks from being able to live in Missouri. Missouri was not a free northern state; geographically, it is north in the United States. Old beliefs die hard, and the racial conflict still raged on.

Kids learned early that there was strength in numbers. A group of white kids that would always pick on this one dumpy black kid named of Melvin. Melvin isolated himself from others by choice, and this made him an easy target. This group of white kids loved easy marks. They would always gang up on Melvin when he was alone. However, the black Guys would rescue Melvin, if they witnessed an attack. They always championed the Ladies.

One night it was a clear cool crisp evening in the neighborhood, until the silence pierced with the sound of gunshot. It was Mr. Goldman. An elderly Jewish Gentleman that lived in our neighborhood. Mr. Goldman owned a jewelry store and he drove a champagne colored Cadillac. This dumb group of boys assumed the owner of this vehicle was black. If they had lived in our neighborhood, they would have known. These kids thrashed Mr. Goldman's car. Hearing the noise, he grabbed his shotgun and headed for the front door. Aiming his gun into the air and pulling the trigger, he scared the white teens and they ran off. My junior year culminated in a school riot. Sadly, blacks against whites. The front of the school was full of kids fighting.

There were many talent shows, and basement parties with the blue, black, or red lights. Barry White, the maestro, was hot; and so was the bump dance. I met Elijah in the crisp new spring of my life. Elijah was a tall bald headed part Cuban that could two-step anyone into the ground. I loved dancing with him as we spun the night away. He was cool and took no shit. Elijah also played bass and sang lead vocals in a local band. I am starting to see a pattern in my choice of men. He initially had thick curly black hair that he shaved off for his cool new look. His mother was half-Indian, who had passed away. Leaving him and his sister to be cared for by their father, a light-skinned Cuban man that worked for the postal service.

Elijah was a senior in high school. We started dating the latter half of my junior year. Things went smoothly and we had great fun. I loved going with him to their gigs and watching the band play. His group even agreed to let me and two other young Ladies dance for the band. It was great. We had costumes made-up and worked hard on our routines. The crowd loved us.

Elijah was real understanding about my being celibate. I somehow could not deal with sex. I did not view it as pleasurable or titillating. I never had a clue that he would betray me.

March of 1974, Bethany called to see how things were going. We had been writing letters, sending postcards, and calling since I left Texas.

"Hi Carmen. How are you?"

"Bethany, I'm fine. How are you?"

"Doing without, but it's got to get better. What is going on girl? Liking the big city?"

"Hell, no. I hate it here. It is too cold, some people are racist, and we do not have as many school activities to participate in, other than sports. I'm not about to run track or play volleyball for these people."

"Really? I thought things were supposed to be better and faster in a big city like that."

"Well, we actually live in a suburb north of St. Louis. They're a bit behind the curve."

"What about the boys?"

"They're okay. I have a new boyfriend by the name of Elijah."

"Oh, that sounds interesting. Tell me more."

We gossiped for the next thirty minutes about what the other was doing and then we hung up.

The summer of 1974, my mother became very ill. The doctors were puzzled as to the etiology of her ailment. She suffered horribly with pain, rash, skin breakage, boils in her head, and hair loss. I so clearly remember hearing her cry at night as I passed their bedroom on my way to the bathroom. She was so kind and loving, why was she suffering? Numerous tests were ran and sleepless nights endured before someone asked her about her hobbies.

Mother loved working in the yard. Planting vegetables and flowers out in the backyard. A lovely vine that grew along the yard, through the chain link fence. It had become rather unruly since mother was not able to give it her usual daily attention. Our neighbor decided to go out and trim things back a bit. He and his wife knew mom was sick and they were very kind and understanding. They were a sweet young white couple who were expecting their second baby any day now.

Mr. Kent and his wife were banging on our front door with a matter of urgency. Daddy answered the door and asked them in and to make themselves comfortable. Mother went to prepare ice tea.

"No, no. Please do not go through any trouble of preparing tea, Mrs. Robertson. I think I know what has caused your illness."

"What? How do you know," my Father gasped.

"I was in the yard today, trimming back the vines. Look at my white tee shirt. It has all these black spots on it."

"I've never known a simple domestic plant to cause such black spots. What do you think it is?"

"I don't know stated Mrs. Kent, but this is surely a breakthrough. Our oldest child was in the yard and he now has a red rash. He's with his grandmother now."

"Yes, his exposure was only for a few minutes. You have been in that yard almost daily for months now. We think you should put some in a plastic bag and take it to your doctor for tests," said Mr. Kent.

"Oh, thank you so much. We appreciate you. We will call him now. Maybe I can run it down there."

"Thank you," my Mother cried.

The Kent's took their leave, wishing my family luck. The plant was the culprit of my mother's illness, and she began a long and slow recovery. She did grow her hair back and stopped wearing wigs. Her complexion was beautiful and glowing again.

My brothers were in and out of trouble over this period in St. Louis for racial fights. Fines and probation for retaliating against the small group of white boys who always cursed my brothers and threw things at their cars. The justice system is so unbalanced. The white kids never received any punishment for initiating conflicts with their acts of hatred. However, the legal defense for my brothers had cost my parents thousands of dollars from their nest egg, and was emotionally damaging for my brothers.

December of 1974, Elijah had proposed and given me an engagement ring. Wow! You could actually see the diamond. However, there were no intentions of marrying until after college, he wanted me to know that his intentions were honorable. His ex-girlfriend was trying feverishly to get him back, but according to him, there was no hope of that. She was a light-skinned girl with hazel eyes and light-brown hair by the name of Renee. At times, I felt inferior to her because of her eyes and hair. Her features were only one type of beauty.

February of 1975, Elijah had planned a special birthday celebration for me, and the evening was to be a surprise. All he would tell me is that we would start with dinner and for me to dress up. I could hardly contain myself.

He had even gone as far as to get special permission from my father to stay out late.

I was so excited. I liked surprises and I knew this would be an evening of shear elegance. In preparation, I did a facial and my own manicure.

Our evening started with a wonderful dinner at a swanky Italian restaurant in downtown St. Louis. The food was delicious and I even had wine, since it was my eighteenth birthday. It was something nice and light that went down smoothly. A recommendation by the maître d'. It was an intimate setting with candle light, white linen tablecloths, and a fresh cut rose in a crystal vase on each table. A small quartet played softly in the background as we enjoyed our meal. There was even a small dance floor for after dinner enjoyment, of which we partook.

We discussed our plans for the future. Elijah had already graduated and spent a year in community college. He had determined that school was not for him and enlisted in the Air Force. He was due to leave at the end of summer.

On the other hand, I had completed modeling school and was doing some work locally. I had also been in a parade as Ms. Black Velvet 1975. My plans were to take science in college in preparation for medical school and model for fun.

It was getting dark when we left the restaurant, about eight-thirty. I was to wear a blind fold to our next stop. I had been dating Elijah for a little over a year now and trusted him. When he removed the blindfold, we had parked at a drive in theatre and the advertisement for concessions was playing.

"A movie?"

"Yes, I thought it would be nice to see a good movie."

"Okay, but what's playing?"

"Be patient. You'll see."

The previews for coming attractions began to play. They were X-rated and turned my stomach. I could not believe he thought bringing me to some low class sex movie would be acceptable. I was appalled.

"Elijah, have you lost your damn mind? How in hell would you think that I would want to see this crap?"

"Well, you aren't giving me any. I figured we had watched other people getting it on and maybe that will make you hot. We have come close before, now it is time to go all the way. You know I have had offers."

"Oh, is that ex-bitch of yours still trying to get in your pants? Fine, I do not give a shit. Go screw her then, if that's all you want."

"Calm down, baby. That is not all I want. I want you. I love you. So, I thought this would help."

"You thought wrong. If you believed that, then you would not have blindfolded me. Get me out of here. I don't want to see this mess."

"First, do you forgive me? I made a mistake and I did not mean to hurt you. I love you."

"Yes, I forgive you. This time, jackass."

"Good, now give me a kiss."

We made up and continued our evening. There was a night concert in Forrester Park. The jazz music under the stars was beautiful. It was one thirty a.m. and my curfew was nearly up. Nevertheless, there was one more stop to make. Elijah stated that his sister had made a birthday cake for me, and she along with his father would be waiting for us. They wanted to sing happy birthday and give me a gift. I wondered if possibly they would be sleep at this hour. He assured me that they were not. Actually, they each had dates of their own and the plan was to meet back at the house at one thirty a.m.

We arrived first. All the lights were out and the house was quiet. Elijah turned on the television and the radio. I hate when he plays both. How can you possibly listen to both? We sat on the couch and kissed a bit.

"Elijah I have to be home by two. Your family is running late. Let's just do this tomorrow, okay?"

"No, Carmen. I am sure they will be here any minute. Please give them a few more minutes. You'll be glad you did."

"Well, this must be some gift. Five more minutes and that is it. You know how my father gets."

We began to kiss again. The kissing led to heavy petting, and before I could say, have mercy, Elijah became an animal. Someone I no longer recognized.

"Elijah. Stop it. You're hurting me."

"It is okay baby, relax."

"No, damn it, stop. Stop!"

I could not control him. He bruised my thighs with his knees pressing them open. As he laid all his weight on top of me, he held my wrists with his large hands. I started to scream and he put one hand around my throat.

"Shut up, Carmen. Why you tripping? You know I ain't gonna hurt you."

"You're hurting me now. Stop!"

A few minutes later, it was over. I was so terrorized and hurt. My body ached and was wet with the fluid of his manhood. I hated him with every fiber of my being, right then, that very moment. I was afraid to move. I laid there almost catatonic for what seemed like forever. When he began to snore, I knew he was asleep and I could get out. His family still had not come home and it was three a.m. I dare not waste time and use his phone. He might awaken.

I left the house and walked home in the snow. It was like a nightmare from which I could not awake. He raped me. He raped me. He loved me, but he raped me. That sorry bastard. He raped me. He hurt me. I had earned my first load of bricks.

I arrived home around three-thirty. As I entered through the front door, a quick hard pain struck my face. My father had slapped me so hard that my head hit the door.

"What time did I tell you to be in? Are you trying to be a slut, my father wailed?"

"You stupid man. Does it make you happy to hit me? You are tough. Hit me again, go ahead and hit me again."

Then my mother interceded with her weakened attempt to hold an angry man back that was twice her size. I quickly ran back out of the front door into the snow. I did not know where I was going. It was a cold night as the brisk wind whisked across my face causing tears to freeze in tracks down my face. I wondered what was happening to me as I walked through the neighborhood in the snow. My heart had been broken twice in one night and my body injured by two men that I thought loved me. One I have known all my life and entrusted with my care since childhood, and the other for the past year and a half. A man I thought I would marry. I then became sick to the stomach at the thought of what had occurred earlier that evening. The pain of the events pierced me like a hot poker. I fell to the ground and emptied the contents of my stomach onto the side of the road.

What can I do? Where can I go? My fingertips were becoming numb, as well as my toes, from the cold night air. It was five a.m. I finally came to the realization that I must return home.

Day was beginning to break as I entered the front door. My father had been out looking for me without success. He had called Elijah's and was told that I was dropped off earlier that morning around one forty-five. The liar. My two brothers and little sister had been sitting at the kitchen table since the moment they awakened with the commotion that had taken place earlier. They were terrified with the wonder of what had happened to me.

"I'm sorry I hit you, Carmen. Go to bed now and we'll talk about this more tomorrow."

"Okay, Daddy. I am sorry, too. I love you and Momma and I didn't mean to worry you."

I took a shower for what seemed like an hour. No matter how hard I scrubbed my skin, I could not wash the stench off. Finally, exiting the shower I went to the sink to brush my teeth. As I raised my arm and with the thick white sleeve of my robe, I began to clear the fogged mirror in a circular motion. What is that? What is that I see? What is that peering back at me from the darkness? I had become someone I no longer recognized. An ugly black void. I had sunk as low as I had ever been in my life. A depth I prayed I would never have to experience again, or would I?

Getting rest was futile. I tossed and turned, but could not find solace. Why did Elijah betray my trust in him? I thought he loved me. Is that what you do to someone you love. If so, I do not want any part of it.

It was around twelve thirty in the afternoon, when I had awakened. Maybe I had three hours of sleep. I could hear my parents talking in the kitchen. First, I went to the bathroom to wash my face.

"Good morning, Momma. Daddy."

"Good morning, Carmen. Take a seat," my Daddy said.

"Are you hungry, baby? Can I make you something to eat?"

"Yes, Momma. I'll take an egg and one slice of toast, please."

"Carmen, what were you thinking coming in so late? How are we supposed to trust you, if you behave this way?"

My father is great in the courtroom, but when it comes to his own family, he does not have a clue.

"I was raped last night."

"What?" my mother gasped as she dropped the frying pan.

My father just stared at me. I pulled up my housecoat to reveal my thighs. They were purple and blue, as well as my wrist. "I said, I was raped," I yelled!

"When did this happen, Carmen? Elijah said he dropped you off this morning around one forty-five."

"He's a liar." As I told them the story, they began to cry. Then my father's sorrow turned to anger.

"Why didn't you tell us this last night, Carmen?"

"Daddy, you didn't give me a chance. Remember, as soon as I came in the door, you hit me; I was lucky enough to be brutalized twice."

My mother cried even more. "I'm going to kill that bastard for touching my baby. Call the police Daddy."

"Now, wait a minute. Let us not lose our heads here. Elijah's a good kid. We have known him for a little over a year now. You two are engaged to be married. Haven't you been together before?"

"No, Daddy we haven't been sexually active before. If you had believed that, you would not have let me go out with him. Momma would have made sure I was on birth control pills. Besides that doesn't give him the right to do what he did."

My mother looked at him bewildered. "Daddy, are you crazy? That fool hurt our baby and I want him arrested, now. How dare you assume your daughter has been promiscuous? We have taken these children to church every Sunday since the day they were born. I am sure some of that teaching has worn off on her. Now, you are going to stand up here and believe the worse without giving her a decent chance. Call the police."

"Honey, listen to me now. It is just going to be his word against hers. They've been going together for over a year. No one is going to believe this. We have a reputation to uphold in this community. The repercussions of this scandal will go a whole lot further and do more harm than good."

"And whose word do you believe, Daddy?"

"Carmen, please. Don't be naïve. You do not know what it is like in a courtroom. The snakes will rip you apart."

"I guess we'll never know. Huh, Daddy. My virtue is expendable. Me, for your ambitions."

I ran to my room and slammed the door. My little sister, who was only eight at the time, came in behind me and laid her head on my back. She has always seemed more like my baby, then my sister. I take her everywhere with me, when I can. My brothers were busy in the basement plotting Elijah's demise.

I refused to see Elijah or accept his calls. One day he came by and caught me outside talking with one of my brother's friends, Elvin. Elijah was still wearing the black eye and broken nose my brothers gave him. Elvin was born deaf, so his speech was different. He wore thick glasses, but was actually cute. He had made a tic-tac-toe set out of brass and silver. It was beautiful. He has always had a crush on me, but I was not into deaf guys. Shame on me.

"Hey, baby. Why haven't you taken my calls?"

"I'm not your baby, and I don't want to speak to you ever again after what you did."

"Carmen, how was what I did so bad? We're engaged to be married."

"So, you think that gives you to right to do with me as you please? You are wrong, you trifling fool. Get the hell away from me."

Elijah picked on Elvin's disability often, but this particular day he was unmercifully cruel.

"What are you doing over here retard? Trying to pick up on my woman?"

"She's my friend and you are bad. You leave her alone."

"Da-da-da-da. The retard can't hardly talk. Can you see out of those thick glasses, huh?"

I ran in the house to avoid contact with Elijah. Elvin kept him from following me. I called to my mother. However, by the time she reached the door from her room, it was nearly over. Elvin had had enough of Elijah's insults. When Elijah tried to hit him, Elvin flipped him. Elijah did not know that Elvin had a black belt in karate. Elvin flipped Elijah all over our front yard. On the last flip, Elijah landed in one of our large bushes out front. All he could do was throw leaves at Elvin. It was hilarious. I called Elvin in and we continued our visit until my brother Louie arrived home.

A few weeks had passed when I became ill. I was nauseated in the mornings and very fatigued. Mother took me to the doctor, who diagnosed me as pregnant. I could not believe it. Pregnant, what am I going to do with a baby? In the final analysis, what I thought did not matter. My parents discussed it and decided that I would have an abortion. From their birds eye view, a baby would ruin my bright future. Not to mention look bad for the family.

I was so scared when my mother and I arrived at the clinic. My father had spoken to Elijah's father. The agreement was that he would pay for the procedure, and keep his son away from me. After, I was lightly sedated the process began. It was still painful. I could see the blood and contents suctioned out into a medium sized clear container. When are they going to finish, it hurts so badly? Soon, it was over and I recovered for an hour while sipping on juice and eating crackers. As I laid on that chaise lounge, I was lost in a world I never knew existed. I was void of any expression. Then there was immense sadness. I had received a prescription for birth control pills, released, and I cried myself to sleep that night. I was now a murderer. I hated myself. My parents did not discuss the matter again. I have now earned my second load of bricks.

Things have been so turbulent. It was a time that I called, controlled chaos. I eventually sat down and wrote Bethany a letter. Time went on and I tried to pull some semblance of a life together. I hated St. Louis and my family has had nothing but bad luck since moving to this place. The only bright spot was that I was going to graduate and leave this Hellhole.

Dear Bethany,

   I hurt so badly way down deep inside. I feel ugly and I can't stand to look at myself in the mirror, for I no longer look the same. I am a murderer of an innocent child. Does God forgive me? Do I forgive myself? I don't know if I can go on. It wasn't even my decision. No one bothered to ask me what I wanted or what I thought. They just want to make sure I have the best future possible and that I don't become another statistic; or are they protecting their reputation. Worried about how it looks to their friends. You know another black woman that didn't get through college, had babies, and is living off the government. Maybe my parents are right. I really don't know right now. All I know is I was betrayed by someone that I thought I loved. That I thought loved me. My God! I hurt so bad deep, deep inside. I just want to die! I miss seeing you and talking to you face to face.

   I cry myself to sleep every night and the next day I have red eyes with dark circles under them. Help me O' Lord not to kill myself. I'm so depressed. I spend no time

*with other friends and I walk through the
school hallways like a zombie.*

*Love your big Sis
Carmen*

CHAPTER 10

The year 1975 was proving to be one hell of a year. Not only for me, but also, for my girls Bethany and TheLetter. When Bethany got my letter, she called me right away to see how I was doing. We both cried for what seemed like an eternity. She went on to tell me how her joyride of a relationship with her first love Greg was coming to a horror story ending. She and Greg had been together since 1973. I just knew if there was such a thing as high school sweethearts, they were it. I cannot say that I was that crazy about how their relationship started, but it seemed to be working out for them. Therefore, as a friend, I felt it best to support Bethany's decision. After all, it was her life and her love.

Now she told me how she had caught him on several occasions with a girl named Sonnie. Of course, Greg always denied that he was messing around with Sonnie, but Bethany said she kept it all in perspective and never trusted him fully because there were too many stories that just did not add up. She told me of how Greg was becoming such a star on the football team that it was all going to his head, and now he was into smoking Mary Jane and doing God knows what else. Although he never smoked in Bethany's presence, because she swore she would never fall into that trap, he also never tried to hide the fact that he got high. Sonnie got high, too. Bethany just rationalized to me that they were two peas in a pod and deserved each other. The only problem was that as Bethany called it quits, Greg would not let go.

That is my girl. Bethany's a straight "A" student, but sometimes lacking in the common sense department. I am glad that this time the only smoke that Greg is blowing is up his own ass! Bethany began crying as she told me of how he had begun stalking her.

"Carmen, girl, I think he has really lost his mind. You know. Got a hold of some bad weed or some shit! I mean I cannot even go out go to dances and parties with my friends. If he is there, he watches me all night long and nobody will dance with me. All the guys stayed away from me like I have a death wish or something. Because, last month, Greg hid in my front yard after a party to see if I was with another guy. I got a ride home with this dude named Sam. He is new to the city and is friends with my cousin Lisa. Do you remember her? Anyway, Sam gives me a ride home and as I was telling him thanks, I see something coming across the front of the car. It was Greg's crazy ass jumping out from beside the hedge next to the curb. Greg walked up to the driver's side and just punched the glass out.

Just like that. Bam-with his fist. I swear he must of been higher than high."

"Wow, Beth. You know I never really got a chance to know him, but I would have never thought he would just go crazy like that. I guess he and Elijah have something in common, huh. I supposed this is Greg's way of making sure that everyone knew that they had better not come around 'messin with his Bet'. We both paused to let all the drama soak in.

"Yeah, girl. I used to think my being 'his Bet' was cute and shit. That nigga's head is blasted and that stupid Sonnie ain't helping matters none at all. She is foul, I tell you. She stays high and does not give a shit about how he dogs her ass in public, running after me and carrying on as if she's not even in the equation. However, as soon as night falls, they are together. I tell you, I love myself more than that! You know she is a nut case sure as the sun rises and sets, as my granddaddy would say."

Bethany went on to tell me about how they had a restraining order against him and that his parents went totally into his stuff and apologized to Beth repeatedly. Mrs. Childs never liked Greg anyway. To her he was too common and his grades were far less than demanded and expected of Bethany and her sisters. I bet Mrs. Childs was secretly thanking God for His divine intervention.

"Carmen, I can't wait to get the hell out of San Antonio. College is calling my name and I am ready to end this freaky situation and move on. As if Greg's fuckin roun' ain't enough, my dad is AWOL again." Talking about salt in the wound.

"Naw, girl! What happened this time?"

"Well, mom caught him with his steady girlfriend, Gwen. That damn Gwen is just like Sonnie's weak ass. Mom met him at the back door with a razor knife. I tell you, that shit was scary, but now it is funny as hell. You should have seen 'em. He was strolling in, cool as ever driving that black deuce and a quarter. However, she jumped up in his face and that man jumped outta his shoes! She was waving that knife around like she was gonna do something, and for a minute she went straight to his crotch. She said something about cutting his balls off and sending them to Gwen!"

Both Bethany and I were laughing now. Somehow, it felt good to laugh some of the hurt away. It was at this moment that we knew that we needed each other more than ever.

"Come on Beth. You've got to watch your mouth. The righteous Mrs. Childs doesn't use that kind of language, being a schoolteacher, preacher's daughter, and upstanding member of the church and community. You need to quit lying on her like that."

"If I'm lying, I'm dying. I tell you she got all up in his face. And he backed down. Next thing I know she was throwing shit all in the driveway and telling him to get the fuck out of her face and don't show back up smelling of some pussy that ain't hers. My mother has lost it this time. My step dad really screwed up. I do not know if they will patch things up this time. So now, she is getting divorce papers drawn up, again. With this life, I'm lucky cursing is all I do."

"Oh, Beth. I am sorry. What is this, divorce number three?"

"Yeah. After three strikes, your ass is O-U-T! I just don't get it. It's like that old Stylistics song, "Break Up to Make Up," I think that's the group. They divorce only to get married again and again and again."

We both decided that drugs had seriously messed up Gregs head and that Mr. and Mrs. Childs were both crazy. Moreover, the whole lot needed an escort out to sea without a map, including Elijah. While I sensed that Bethany was not afraid of Greg, she was afraid of what he was doing to her life. I worried about her. Her family destroyed; and, her sisters were both off doing their own thing and she was a real loner sometimes. She was so young. She started school at four because she was so smart, but that sometimes was more of a disadvantage for her with everyone else being so much older. Nevertheless, she was strong. You to give it to her recognition for that.

I heard Mrs. Childs say something to Beth in the background. God, I hope she was not eavesdropping. Boy, would she be pissed. Bethany got back on the phone.

"Hey girl, I've got to go. Mom, I mean "Mother", said that Chad is here to study for his Spanish III exam. She now insist that I call her 'Mother' cause mom sounds too common. She is such a trippin wannabe sometimes. Anyway, you remember Chad from down the street, don't you? He's playing "B" ball now and is getting all the girls. Can you believe that? He is lookin' kinda' good with that bad ass fro, I must say. Too bad he is only a junior."

Bethany sounded like her old self again and I felt better, too. As we ended our conversation, we vowed to stay in touch. We missed each other so much and life was really dealing us some funky hands. To think, all this chaos and we were still in high school. Life is supposed to be balanced and well lived. With all this crap going on, the future has to be better. We could only ponder what would life be like once we began college. As Bethany put it, "If this high school relationship bullshit was the first act, then the next act is going to either be a cake walk or like shitting bricks."

TheLetter had fallen hard and fast in love with a young man by the name of Cisco. They married after a short courtship and moved to Minneapolis with his family, June of 1973. The marriage ended almost as quickly as it had begun due to his infidelities. I guess coming home to find him in bed with another woman was her limit.

TheLetter would become involved with one short dumpy older man after another. Devoting herself whole-heartedly to them, only to be disappointed. By their phobia of the ultimate committed relationship, marriage.

She finally felt as though she had found the prefect mate, though he lingered away from the wedding chapel. He was nice enough but had plenty of baggage of his own. TheLetter would deem herself the savior of thrashed souls and believed her love could quench any hidden thirst he had and allow him to relinquish all insecurities about relationships.

TheLetter met Damian in August of 1976 at a Minneapolis nightclub. The relationship floated along. He took her out frequently and paid all the time. Though signs of jealousy would surface, TheLetter viewed it as cute and let his remarks go unchallenged.

Within six months, they moved in together. The only thing this accomplished was having one rent. TheLetter was so blindly in love with Damian Stephens or the idea of a happy marriage. Regardless of all the signals, late night pages on Damian's voice mail, and their arguments, TheLetter stayed with Damian. She even forgave him for the one time he slapped her, and the time he choked her. For a future attorney, she was not too bright.

Chalking them up to mere misunderstandings. After which, they would indulge in heightened passions to make up. I tried numerous times to explain to TheLetter that this was unhealthy behavior and could not end on a positive note. That these were the very behaviors that led to murders of passion. Only God could have envisioned the horrid fate that would follow.

I decided to call TheLetter. We needed to catch up a bit. I had not yet told her about the pregnancy and abortion. I wanted to give her my new address at school. I was due to leave this weekend. The phone rung for what seemed like ten times; then, the answering machine picked up. Where could she be? It is three a.m. there. I began to leave a message, when she picked up the phone sounding as if she had run a marathon.

"Hang on, I'm here. Just a minute."

"TheLetter? Are you all right?"

"Yes, who's calling?"

"Who's calling, are you going senile? What, you don't recognize my voice anymore?"

"Carmen. Of course, I recognize your voice. I'm sorry girl, it's late and I've been working real hard lately."

"I'll say. It's after three a.m. Do you usually work this late, TheLetter?"

"No, but I've taken on extra caseloads to help with expenses around here."

"Let's talk about that TheLetter. What expenses? You are a law clerk for a major firm, in your last year of college, preparing for law school. In addition, your grandfather left you boo-coo dollars. What expenses, TheLetter?"

"Well, it's Damian."

"What about Damian? Last I heard he was a grown man with a job, not your baby."

"Carmen please, don't get judgmental on me, otherwise this conversation is over."

"Okay, fine. I'm sorry. Go ahead."

"Damian quit his job two months ago. He said that he was not being; or, treated fairly at the plant. That caused him to go into depression and he started spending time at the track. When he lost all his savings, he signed IOU's. Those IOU's eventually totaled over a hundred thousand dollars. Half of that to loan sharks. The only way I could get them off his back was to promise that I'd pay it. They agreed to that, but it wiped my savings out. I mean, I've only been on the job for less than a year."

"Girl, are you freaking crazy. Can't you see he's playing you for a fool? Loan sharks my ass. Just let them eat him then. How do you know they weren't some home boys from around the block?"

"Come on Carmen. Damian wouldn't do that. He loves me for God's sake."

"Don't put God in this mess. That man loves you about as much as he did when he slapped you. Remember that. That lazy piece of slug needs to get his ass out of your bed and make his own way."

"Carmen, you promised not to be judgmental."

"I'm not being judgmental, TheLetter. I'm telling you the truth about your situation. A truth you obviously don't want to hear. Girl this man is going to run you in the ground. You've got to get him out of there."

"Please, enough about me. What's going on with you, Carmen?"

"Well, I'm getting ready to go away to college this weekend. Sam Houston State University in Huntsville, Texas. Bethany and I graduated high school this year, and I'm finally getting out of this hell hole."

"Wait a minute. Isn't that where one of the prisons is?"

"Yes, just a few short blocks away actually. It was kind of creepy to see, and sad all at the same time."

"Trust me they did something to get in there."

"There's more. I broke up with Elijah. He raped me on my eighteenth birthday. I became pregnant and had an abortion."

"What? Are you all right? Why didn't you call me?"

"I was having trouble dealing with it myself. Didn't feel much like talking. You know. Anyway, I'm better, now. Just not sure I want another man to touch me."

"That's understandable. However, it will pass. You just need time to heal."

"I guess so. I just wanted to holler at you girl and give you my new school address; then, I have to finish packing."

"Okay, go ahead."

We chatted for a few more minutes and then said our goodbyes. I cut on my radio and a song by the Dramatics was playing, "*What You See Is What You Get.*" A sadness filled my heart. Not just for myself, but for my friend. I felt as though she had willingly sentenced herself to a life of drudgery.

DO YOU KNOW ME?

Do you know me? My heart, my soul,
my spirit?
Who am I to you or to myself?

Who am I? What am I? Am I
A beautiful woman, because
I have socially acceptable features by
mans account?
Or, am I beautiful because I love myself
and others as they are?
I am a seeker through this place we call
earth.
What I seek is a higher plane.
A spiritual understanding.
A place where we aid each other
With no thought of repayment.

Do you listen as I speak?
Do you hear my heart as it cries out?

Carmen

CHAPTER 11

My debut into collegiate society was not conventional. It was actually a bit risqué. The lobby of the dormitory was large and nicely decorated. It even had a baby grand piano and two small brass chandeliers, hanging from the ceiling. The rooms, however, were not as spacious. There were two twin beds, two average sized closets, and one large workstation with shelves that extended across half the wall. We also had a bathroom with two sinks and a shower, which we shared with our suitemates. My roommate was Marletta Brown, my cousin. Our suitemates were Regina and Wanda. They were two of the six girls that came from Lufkin, Texas. A small country town about one hour north of Huntsville. They were all great and we became fast friends. When we did not have dates, we played cards.

Marletta and I decided to go down to the dorm cafeteria for breakfast before getting dressed for the day. Since it was an all-girls dorm, we felt it would be no problem going down in our baby doll nighties, fluffy house shoes, and our bonnets full of those big plastic rollers.

We giggled and chatted all the way down the hall, the stairs, and right up to the cashier to show our student identification cards. We did not realize anything was wrong until a deafening silence fell upon our ears. As we slowly looked up and we were hit with the realization that there were boys in that cafeteria, also.

"Boys," we shouted. We tried futilely to cover ourselves and back out of the cafeteria. As the crowd hooted and howled to egg us on, we ran back up the stairs to our room. There was no doubt that everyone knew who we were. We did not go down to eat and stayed in our room all day. The Luftkin 6, Regina, Kathleen, Wanda, Judy, Willette, and Olivia brought us food. I just wanted to know from the Lord, how many more mistakes would I be making?

A few days later after breakfast, Marletta and her new male friend had an upper classman that they wanted me to meet. Supposedly, he was very interested. I wandered if it was because of my cafeteria escapade. His name was T.C. Grey-cloud. T.C. was a six foot two inch dark bowlegged masterpiece. His father was a tall handsome Indian, cool, kind, and laid back. His mother, a very dark skinned holy roller. Said to be in church every possible waking moment, tapping on her tambourine, and praying for the Holy Ghost, so she could speak in tongues.

T.C. had his mother's silky smooth complexion and his father's hair. Long black hair that he wore in two French braids on each side of his head. All the girls on campus sought his attention. I could care less, since I really was not sure that I liked men. This man asked me to be his Lady, to which, I responded, no. On day seven, he made me an offer. Give him three weeks to make me happy and I will not be sorry. If I do not find it to my liking then simply dump him.

My first year in college was happy. We were one of the hottest couples on campus. We made most of the parties and danced until we could not stand anymore. The best parties were by my big brothers, the Alpha Kappa Alphas'.

I had pledged Alpha Angels. There was not much to it and T.C. watched the big brothers every move. The night that I completed pledging was *Going Over*. I played chess, how boring, but no one wanted to anger T.C.

The Step Show for all new Greeks and non-Greeks was great. We had just gone over the week before. I was tail dog for my line and our song was Flashlight, by Parliament. We came in through the main front doors, and had these different colored lights. We had worked hard on our routine and the show was a great success. My name was Lady Ecstasy.

Summer break came and went. I was a bit concerned about T.C.'s fidelity. Word had reached me that one of his old girlfriends from high school had been driving up to campus trying to woo him back. I needed to investigate for myself. I had to look him in his eyes when I asked the question.

According to T.C., this female intruder had tried her wiles to no avail. I told him if she wanted him bad enough, she would get pregnant to get him, so, watch it. A month into my sophomore year, the fall of 1977, T.C. called on me at my dorm. When I entered the lobby, it was unusually full of people. T.C. was waiting for me at the piano.

As I sat with him on the bench, he began to play a slow beautiful love ballad. Suddenly, he stopped, looked me in my eyes, got down on one knee, and proposed.

"Married, married, I-I don't know, T.C."

"Carmen, I love ya' girl. You're so different and unique. Please say yes and be my wife."

I glanced around the room as everyone stood with anticipation. "Yes, T.C. I'll marry you."

There was thunderous applause and congratulations as he placed the ring on my finger, and we hugged and kissed. I was so happy at that very moment. This man was true to his word, and even waited six months to be intimate with me. However, was I ready for marriage?

T.C. was a senior and had great connections through his fraternity brothers. He was getting an engineering degree and had a great career awaiting him in Houston. My first sophomore semester was off with a bang, and I was going to pledge Alpha Kappa Alpha (AKA). We had a great future ahead of us.

It was November of 1977 when Bethany called.

"Hello there, speak to me."

"Carmen, is that part of your college training?"

"Hey, Bethany. What's going on girl?"

"Not much. I got your letter about this engagement and just wanted to know if you'd lost your mind? You know there are a lot of loose screws running around."

"No, Beth. I haven't lost my mind. I do love him, and the wedding won't be until after I graduate."

"I see. Carmen, don't you think it's strange that the proposal came right after you confronted him with your suspicions?"

"I did think of that, of course. However, getting married wouldn't fix anything, if the rumor were true. Sure, he's a man, but he's not that stupid. But, I'm not sure I'll actually go through with it. As we know, even a lie has some bit of truth."

"Hmmm. I guess so. How's pledging going?"

"I got off line."

"What, are you crazy? Why?"

"Well, I had been in the clinic for the past two and a half weeks with an intense strep throat infection. When they called my parents, momma told them to give me an enema and cod liver oil. That's her cure for everything. My line sisters were giving me flack for not suffering with them."

"You were suffering, Carmen. Maybe that enema would have helped you think clearly. Besides, I thought we were going to be sorority sisters."

"I know. But I guess they didn't see it that way. And we are sisters no matter what, Bethany."

"What about your big sisters?"

"They were cool. They visited with and without my line sisters. They didn't want me to drop. Remember they sought me out to be an AKA."

"Yeah, I remember. Which meant you have what it takes. They saw something in you that made them want you to be a part of their sorority. Being a member of a sorority could mean a lot for a successful future. Carmen, remember during your interview, when one of them asked you if you'd try to get even with them for something that might happen during pledging and you said, yes."

"Hell, yeah! I said that I would hunt them down like a dog and make them pay."

"Girl, you are crazy, and they still put you on line."

"You know Bethany, I never understood why people feel they have to be part of some big name organization to be of value. I joined the Angels to hang out and party. There are many times when I just want to be by myself regardless of what anyone thinks or feels. I just want to be me. A unique individual. Am I any better or worse with a title?"

"No I guess not. However, you have always been that way Carmen. A strong and independent person who does what she wants, and says what she feels, regardless of what someone else thinks. We all have to do what is right for us, you know. I am a legacy. I mean my mom pledged AKA. and it's only natural that I keep it going in the family. I know she's a stone trip, but she means well and all. I had to have a 2.8 G.P.A. in order to pledge. The Sorors here only took potentials with a 3.0 or better. They are making me study my ass off, but you know, that's what I need. All this party stuff can get out of hand here on the hill. When it's all over, I'm sure I'll be called a snob. However, I really don't give a damn cause I'll be an educated sister on a mission to success! Doing it the AKA way...Hey!"

"Don't blame it on pledging. You've always been a snob, Beth."

"So, like I said we do what feels right, and only you can control your destiny and make choices that are right for you. You'll be okay. And I AM NOT A SNOB, I just have standards!"

"Yeah, except when it comes to personal relationships with the opposite sex. I tend to take on their desires and wants as my own. Instead of speaking out from the start and saying no. But, that is going to change."

"Carmen. I won homecoming queen. I'll be in the homecoming parade in three weeks."

"Congratulations, girlfriend. You are beautiful. Both inside and out. They picked the right person. I bet your big sisters are proud, too."

"Yeah, they are. Hey, remember our budget. I'll call you next week, or just see you for Christmas break. Bye!"

THE LIMIT

To hold and cherish the thing you love,
You treat your dog with a lighter glove.
Give me all you have he bellows out.
And when you are drained,
I'll clamor, more. No doubt.
Mind of my mind, rib of my rib.
Your soul mate, why do you disrespect and hate.
What would it take for love redeemed.
To glitter like gold in God's calming stream.
Hold my hand, pull me close.
Be my protector and guide me through.
Show me true love as never before,
and I will respect, nurture, and support you.
Together we can reach all heights.
The sky, the sun, the stars, if it's your delight.

Carmen

CHAPTER 12

Christmas break in San Antonio was wonderful. TheLetter flew in and we got together as we always did. I also missed seeing my family, especially my little sister Liz. Once the preliminaries were out of the way, the girls and I hit club Illusions, in downtown San Antonio. Everyone in college would be home for the holidays.

On Fridays' we hit the clubs, Saturdays the malls, and Sundays the roller rink. Things were especially live and the boys got cuter. Ah yeah, the skate line was back. One thing we loved was to wear the colored bandanas around our legs, and a sweat rag in your pocket. At that time, it was just cool and had nothing to do with being in a gang. It had to do with the originator, Jimi Hendrix, Mr. Cool himself.

Earth, Wind, and Fire's song, "Get Away," was one of the crowd favorites. We would go as fast as we could in a line around that rink, fancy footwork and all. It never took long to work out a line routine, and there were those who had routines they had worked on for weeks. They would get in the center by two, threes, or fours to flash. This was not a time to be on the floor, if you could not skate. It is amazing how much fun people get out of going in circles.

My younger brother by two years, Kennard, often went with us. He was the only one I knew that skated like Frankenstein and he did not fall down. By the end of the night, my feet and legs ached, but it was still fun.

It was midnight, and the rink was closing. While on the way to the car, trying to decide on a restaurant for breakfast, a voice came out of nowhere.

"Carmen? Is that you?"

"Yes? Bugeye?"

"Yeah. Except I prefer my real name, Leon."

"Oh, sure. What's going on?"

"Not much. Playing football at U.T. in Austin. How have you been? When did you get back?"

"I've been all right. I'm in school at Sam Houston State. My family moved back last summer."

"Wow! That's wonderful. I've missed you. Maybe we can get together sometimes?"

"Well, I don't know, Leon. My schedules pretty full. Besides, I'm engaged. I'll see you around, okay."

"Yeah, all right. Take care of yourself."

The girls and I jumped in the car and headed for the Waffle House.

"Leon looked good, huh Carmen?"

"Yeah, he is really muscular, TheLetter. I wonder if he got quarterback? You know his dream was to play for the Dallas Cowboys? Why did they call him bugeye? His eyes aren't big at all?"

"I don't know, Carmen."

"I know, but I never really talked to him. He was always so quiet."

"Whatever. He's muscular, boring, and still blue black."

"Bethany, I'm shocked. Is that all you care about, a brothers complexion, the type of car he drives, and how much money he makes? You are so shallow."

"And you are so naïve, TheLetter. You can't get anywhere in this world without more education, and connections. If you're going to be with someone, be with somebody that's going somewhere. Leon is too dark, and he is from the ghetto. His family has no real history. They're just there."

"Bethany, how do you know where he's going in life. You never spent more than ten minutes talking to him. Just because his family hasn't achieved much financially or scholarly doesn't mean he's condemned to the same life. God. And you know what else? You're a damn racist. A racist against your own people who don't pass that old paper sack test. Girl, you need to wake up, because you're lost somewhere."

"I'm not a racist, TheLetter. I just know what it takes to make it in this world. Besides, I'm black, also. So, I can't be a racist."

"Beth, darling. Not all racist are white," I sighed. "And just how is it that you know what it takes to make it in this world? You're all of nineteen!"

"Let's just say I know, Carmen. I've had the privilege of good upbringing. Plus, the very definition of racism is that a person using their power or position to systematically oppress. So there you have it. I am not a racist. You can call me snob all you want if that is how you want to define it. I have standards."

"Well, if the benefit of good upbringing is being a snob, then I'm glad I don't have it," TheLetter said.

"Ladies, ladies, please. You two always get into these arguments. Shut it up, or I'll kick you right here on the curb. Now, can we just go in and eat? Please?"

Life's Scar

Red, warm with life's fluent stream.
Breath of life renewing its flow.
Warmth, comfort, nurturing to grow.
Love, protection, guidance abound.

With hate, disappointment, lies come down
scarring the fertile ground.
Dull, wither, dark, decay
Betrayal was their delight.

Dishonor, distrust, destroy, and maim
Black cold death slowly crawls

Carmen

CHAPTER 13

January 1978, Christmas break was over and everyone was checking back into the dorms. However, I signed a lease to rent a room from a middle-aged woman that lived about five miles from campus. It was a nice country area and she always seemed to be at church, so, I had a lot of privacy. My bedroom and bathroom were at the front of the house, off the living room, dinette, and kitchen. Her bedroom and bath were in the back past the kitchen.

The Lufkin 6 had rented apartments closer to campus. We had kept in touch over the holidays. When there was not a party, the girls and I would continue our ritual of playing cards at their apartment. T.C. came out to help me settle in before going to a fraternity meeting at six p.m. Soon after he left the phone rang. It was Kathleen.

"Carmen?"

"Hey, girl. What's going on?"

"I have something to tell you. Are you alone?"

"Yes. Go ahead."

I listened intently and then hung up the phone. Kathleen was of the highest integrity. I could not easily dismiss anything she had to say. T.C. was due back that night for dinner, and I needed to handle my business. I continued to put my clothes away, showered, and fixed a chef's salad for my dinner. A knock came at the door around nine p.m.

"Well. Hello tall dark and handsome. Come on in, I've been waiting for you."

"Hi, baby," he said as he kissed me on my lips ever so gently and sensuously.

M-m-m. Lord, tell me I am not about to do what I think I am about to do. "T.C., the grapevine dialed me up tonight and word is that your little chicky from high school past has been up hear a few times during the holidays."

"That's some grapevine, Carmen. Okay, yeah. She's been running up here trying to get me back every chance she had. You know the type, desperate. What's for dinner?"

"Oh, no. My Black King. There's no dinner for you and I've already eaten. How dare you act like it's all her fault. You must have done something to make her keep sniffing around."

"But, baby I…."

"Shut it up, T.C. This is what's going to happen. You are going to get the hell out of my face, go handle your business, and don't come back until you do."

"So, what you trying to say? You breaking up with me, Carmen?"

"Well, it's good to see that your college education is paying off. Good looking and smart. Come on, baby, you've gotta go. Yes, we're breaking up until this mess is cleared up. I don't have time for bullshit and it's starting to stink around here."

"Fine! I'll make sure she stays away. I love you, Carmen and I don't want to be without you. I'll prove to you that I am innocent and the grapevine is lying on me."

"Yeah, Yeah. Get to stepping now." I opened the front door for him to leave. T.C. looked like a love sick puppy that had just been scolded. "Oh! I know you said you're innocent. But, if the heifer wants you bad enough, she'll get pregnant to catch you. So, watch your back."

I stood my ground and did what I had to do. No man is going to use me. Love or no love. However, I could not fool myself. I was more angry and hurt. Nonetheless, I do not play. Besides this was a busy time with classes starting and all the rush parties. I enjoyed my new liberties. I danced until my legs felt limp. There was this tall mocha cutie by the name of Beau, who wanted to date me. He even had a beauty mole over the end of his right upper lip, ouch. Finely trimmed moustache and smooth skin. He was a good man, committed and caring. I just was not ready for another relationship, yet. I was attracted to him. However, when we kissed, there were no sparks. On one level, I felt like I was committing a form of incest. Unfortunately, he was not the man for me. It was good to know there are some gems out there. Like panning for gold. Most times you get fool's gold, and sometimes you get the real thing. At least, he was not like some men who had the IQ of an ant and whose idea of fun was sitting on the porch, watching the cars go by. A cheap patent leather.

The skate parties were fun, also. I had a new light blue jumper with white fringe trim sewn down each side of the pant legs. Oh, I was hot. T.C. left messages on my answering machine and came by every chance he got, leaving notes and money on the door. Telling me how much he loved me. Declaring his innocence and begging me to accept the ring back.

After about three weeks, I was feeling a bit down. The thought of male scum brought Damian to mind. I developed a desire to speak with TheLetter. She is so sweet and compassionate. Her kind words could assuage my pain.

After what seemed like forever, someone picked up the phone.

"Hello?"

"This is Carmen. May I speak with TheLetter?"

"Oh, hey Carmen, baby?"

"Fool. Don't call me baby. You don't know me like that. Where's TheLetter?"

"Why you gotta be so mean? We should be friends, since I'm seeing your girl."

"I'm not in the habit of making friends with leaches. Is TheLetter in or not?"

"Ouch! No, she hasn't come home from work, yet."

"Why is it that you're always there, Damian? Why is that?"

"I'm taking care of home. Besides, I've been looking."

"From where the couch?" Then a females' voice sheared through the phone.

"Come on baby. Hang up."

"You sorry piece of shit. You have another woman in TheLetter's bed? What are you doing with TheLetter's money, Damian? I know you didn't get in debt with loan sharks. You don't strike me as being that stupid."

"You're right. Maybe you should be the lawyer. My wife and I are enjoying a nice life style thanks to my baby TheLetter."

"Not for long slug. I'm going to tell her."

"Go ahead. She won't believe you. She's in love and I have her wrapped around my finger. Besides, I'll just deny speaking with you, and tell her you're jealous of our relationship."

"You better watch it Damian. You know people come up missing every day."

I slammed the phone down. Instead of my friend calming me, her concubine infuriated me. Our world was confusion, pain, and chaos. That social rag-a-muffin was two timing her. After a little investigation and a few phone calls, I discovered a lot. Instead of paying off his debts with the racetrack, he was paying rent in a lavish chicken coop condominium by the river. All thanks to TheLetters naïve generosity. H-m-m-m. I need to make a few more calls.

DON'T TELL

I didn't want to tell nobody, I didn't want to let my feelings show
I didn't want to tell nobody, so I had to let him go
I just had to let him go.

He said his heart was mine, He put it on the line
He just had to let me know
His heart was mine, He thought it was time
He just had to let me know, He just had to let me know.
I didn't want to tell nobody, I didn't know how to let my feelings show
Though his heart was mine, body and soul
I couldn't put mine on the line
I just have to let you go, I'm sorry but I have to let you go.

Carmen

CHAPTER 14

Weeks had passed and Bethany had not called. I had been leaving messages with her roommates. It was apparent that her attention was elsewhere. Possibly, Bethany was investing more time into her new relationship then she said she would. She had a new boyfriend, Tony Simmons. He was several years older than Beth and had graduated from Southern University in Baton Rouge. He was a professional baseball player for the Mariners, and drove a gold Corvette. Their relationship intensified once Bethany became an A.K.A. Word was that he had been by her side every waking moment. According to one of her roommates, Bethany's campus related activities and outings had decreased. Her list of friends had shortened, and her schoolwork was suffering. I know her phone calls and letters had decreased, as well. It would seem that this young man was controlling her by eliminating her social contacts, and I did not like it. Something was cooking and it did not smell good.

That is the way it worked, as isolation from friends and family deepened, Bethany and Tony's ill relationship accelerated. Beth and

Tony met at a party in Houston. Since Beth's parents' last breakup, her father had moved to Houston and she usually made the forty-five mile trek from Prairie View to Houston each weekend after classes were over. She spent much of the weekend partying with Sorors from Texas Southern University (TSU) and University of Houston (UH) and crashing at her dad's place.

At one such party, Beth met Tony, who was also a Greek. An Omega, or "Q-Dog" as more commonly known. He had a build like a male brick house. Jet Black hair, chiseled muscular body, and skin that was so ebony that he could be absorbed by the night. Beth did not usually go for the darker guys, because her mother was rather color struck and always encouraged her girls against darker-skinned boys. Of course, Mrs. Childs was simply a product of what most southern blacks fell victim to long ago. Self-hatred and creating false barriers along color lines. Sometimes, I do not know how Mr. Childs lasted as long as he did.

Tony had a dark side that was so unlike any other guy Bethany had known. Part of this was due to his age and extensive experience with the ladies. He certainly had his share of groupies. However, he saw Bethany as different. She was much more refined than most girls her age and he could not believe at first that she was still in school. Deep down inside, I think he really liked or maybe even loved her, but because he was a macho jock, having several women was the "modus operandi" in order to keep his macho jock status. This chipped away at her soul and individuality. Abuse in any form or language is still abuse. However, one particular night, Bethany yelled, Whoa. She realized that she did not have to take it anymore. She would realize that she did not have to have a man in spite of how he handles her body, mind, and spirit.

"Hey, Beth. This is your man. Baby, tell me how much you miss me."

"Tony, I didn't expect you to call so late. You know it's a school night. Where are you? Are you O.K.?"

"I'm O.K. now that I am talking to you. Why don't you get out of that bed and come downstairs and show me how much you love me."

"What? Where are you?"

"I'm in the lobby and if you are not down here in the next five minutes, I'll take that as a sign that you are either too busy for me or you have somebody else you're playing with on the side."

"I'm on my way."

Yep. Just like that, to Tony she runs. They hugged and kissed downstairs. Curfew was at eleven p.m. It was ten forty-five when Tony arrived.

"Tony, you know I don't have much time. I thought you weren't coming back from Houston until Friday morning. It is Wednesday. How did you get out of your meeting so quickly?"

"Well, baby. It's like this. I got up and I said Beth's birthday is Thursday. If I am home on Wednesday, we can welcome that birthday in style. Go get your things. I got us a room for the night."

"Tony, what about class. You know I am trying to get a degree here *and* graduate with honors. That is unless you are planning to take care of me."

"Hell girl. That's what I'm trying to do right now!"

"Tony, you know that is not what I am talking about. I mean that…"

"Beth. Stop trippin' and get your gear. I ain't got all night. Shit, a nigga flies all the way from Florida and this is all you can do? I guess you are not the woman I thought you were. So, little girl, run on back to your bed. We both know how you have to get your sleep."

"Shit, Tony. I'll be right back."

On her way up to pack, Beth knew this situation was not right. She had a major test on Friday and assignments to turn in tomorrow and the Professor will not take any late work.

"Shit. What am I gonna do? Tony could not have shown up at a worse time. Damn. Sometimes I wonder if he even cares if I finish and get my degree. He ought to understand that much, hell he did go to college. These men can be so controlling and selfish." Bethany reached her room and one of her roommates turned on the light.

"So, Romeo's back in town, and look at you, grabbing all your shit ready to take a sneak outta here. His shit must be gold plated."

"Shut up, Sabrina. It's nothing like that."

"Right, right," Sabrina smiled and they both laugh.

"Hey, you bitches shut the fuck up," scolded the other roommate.

"Oh hell, go to bed."

"Sabrina, see what you did. You woke up Lisa. Damn, Lisa, er'body does not appreciate being called bitches. I wasn't raised like that. So could you please…"

"Could I please what, bitch? Leave your ass alone so you can hurry up and fuck that Mandingo nigga. Yeah, I guess so. Cause word is he is all hung and shit like a race horse. Can't blame you for that."

"Lisa!" shouted Sabrina.

"Oh, that is it. You never liked me and now your nasty, foul, ghetto trash talking is getting on my last nerve. You better be glad I don't have time for this. I will take care of you when I get back." Bethany grabbed her purse and gathered her toiletries.

"Yeah, if you can walk when you get back. I heard the last bitch he had had to get a hysterectomy or some shit like that. Heard he went through her shit like Roto Rooter!"

Beth could not take it anymore. She dropped her things, walked right up to Lisa and slapped her as she started to sit up in bed. The slap startled Lisa, but she half expected it. Lisa jumped up and the fight was on. Sabrina got out of the way and screamed as Lisa reached for a lamp and crashed it into Bethany's back. If Bethany had not turned, the lamp would have struck her in the face. Glass was all over the floor and Bethany slipped and fell, cutting herself all over. Blood was everywhere. By this time, the hallway was full of gawkers. Sabrina ran downstairs and got Tony. She told him what was going on and he ran up the stairs. He stopped at the door, seeing Bethany like that really shocked him. He looked at Lisa and rushed towards her.

"I am going to kill you, you black-ass bitch. You have fucked up Bethany and now I'm gonna fuck you up so bad that your momma won't know which end came out first."

Tony grabbed Lisa. She screamed, "Come on mother fucker, come on! He slapped her so hard, she spun around and hit the floor and went out cold."

The campus police showed up and arrested Tony. Bethany rushed to the hospital. Thank God, most of her cuts were only superficial. Nevertheless, she did have two that required stitches on her left thigh. Lisa came to, and escorted to the hospital for observation. The dorm was buzzing about the goings on. Tony explained things to the campus police, who called in Sabrina as a witness. Before Sabrina was questioned, an officer by the name of Wright, was completing his shift. He recognized Tony, a professional baseball player for the Mariners, and asked what was going on. After a conference with the other officers, Officer Wright told Tony he could go. However, he would have to consider the campus off limits. He explained that he could not blame him for what he did. Lisa can file assault charges if she forced the issue.

"Tony, I've been following your career. I know how these women can work the nerves. So, the best thing to do is to forget the girl. You must have a thousand women out there lined up. What is this girl anyway, five to six years younger than you; and, she is still in school, man. I know how we like these young and tenders sometimes, but this time consider yourself lucky. Don't let me see you down here again son or things may turn out differently."

"Thanks Officer. I understand, but..."

"No buts. Do you read me?"

"Yeah."

"I'll handle this Lisa character. I think I have already had a few complaints on her anyway."

Tony left. He wanted to make things up to Bethany, but maybe the officer was right. Bethany may have a woman's body and mature looks and certainly the brains, but she was young. "Shit, this sneaking in and out of dorms is getting old anyway. I need a real woman who can meet my needs. This college trip is too much for me anyway. I need to concentrate on my career. I should have stayed my ass in Florida. I have a woman there who ain't got no other priority but me." He got in his corvette and burned rubber toward the campus gates. "Ain't shit but trouble on these college campuses any way."

Bethany got back to the room around four a.m. The dorm supervisor met her in the room. She explained the arrangements to have her moved to another dorm. The supervisor further explained to her that this would all go in her records and that if anything like that happened again, she could forfeit her scholarship. They agreed that calling her parents was not necessary. Beth was relieved about that.

Bethany began packing. Some of her Sorors came to help-out after hearing about all the commotion. "Damn, why did all this have to happen? All he wanted was to see me on my birthday. That Lisa! I hate her low-life project ass. Where in the hell did all that hate come from anyway? I just don't understand some of these women down here at all"

One of her Sorors grabbed a packed bag, headed out the door and said, "Come on Beth. Let's just get your stuff and get out before that crazy Lisa shows up and we all go to jail."

The day after the fight, Beth called the campus police to see what happened to Tony. An officer told her he was let go and not charged and that was that. She was relieved upon hearing the news. *So, he's all right, it's my birthday, I'll hear from him tonight. I know he has something special for me*, she thought to herself. Her birthday came and went and then days go by, still no word from Tony. Bethany called Tony's apartments in Houston and Florida every day. He never answered. She wrote him. He never answered. Sabrina called her about two weeks later in her new room to check on her.

"I waited to call you. I sort of feel that this is my fault. If I hadn't started talking, Lisa would have stayed asleep and..."

"Forget it Sabrina. Lisa had it out for me the day she laid eyes on me. We both know that. Thanks though for the kindness."

"Oh Beth, I am so sorry about everything. I mean I know Tony must be feeling so bad about everything."

"Tony? I haven't heard from him since that night. He didn't even call me for my birthday. That bastard..." Bethany cried for the first time. It was the first time she had spoken his name since her birthday. She realized how much she missed him, but she hated him too. She had crossed that thin line between love and hate.

"Beth, I didn't know you had not heard from him. I guess he took Officer Wright seriously."

"What are you talking about?" Sabrina told her all about what happened at the campus police station."

"You mean he just did what they said? He didn't even have the decency to call or write me. He knows where I am every weekend and he could not make his way over there to my father's house? I do not get it. He told me he loved me, but he gave up on us just like that!"

She bursts into more tears and sobs. Sabrina cannot take it. Now she really was sorry that she called. She hung up leaving Bethany alone in her sorrow.

Dear Carmen,

   I know I haven't written or spoken to you in awhile. At first it was because I was so busy with my so called love life. Boy, just when you think you know someone, they turn out to be totally different. I am single and free once again. Tony and I are history. I don't even want to rehash it, but let's just say that once again my choices have turned out to be totally wrong. I just don't get it. My birthday was so messed up. I could use some R and R. Let's meet in Houston two weeks from Friday. I'll call you that Friday evening at your Uncle's. I'll stay with my father as per usual. Call TheLetter and see if she can make it.

Love Beth,

P.S. I need a new pair of shoes

CHAPTER 15

Our occasional weekends in Houston were becoming a monthly ritual. April 1978, three months had passed, and no rumors or innuendos were circulating about T.C. and his high school pal. I missed him. It was a Friday afternoon when T.C. called. He wanted me to know that he was going home for the weekend. I asked if I could go. By this time, I was missing home and the family experience. No matter what I said, he did not think it was a good idea, because he would be busy working with his father. I finally settled for him bringing back a plate of his mother's home cooking with dessert.

T.C. returned on Sunday evening as promised. He bought me a large plate of food, too. Man, it was great. Smothered chicken over rice, greens, homemade rolls, and peach cobbler. I ate like a little piggy. We enjoyed a movie, and then retired to my bedroom.

I had missed being with him and he was always so gentle and kind when we made love. After my rape, I did not think I would ever be with a man again. It did not matter to T.C. in the beginning that we waited six months before making love. He took it like a Champ when I put his head in a lock between my legs to squeeze the life out of him, because he tried to go below my navel. I slowly began to enjoy sex and a man's touch.

The sun's morning rays woke us as they played across our faces.

"Good morning, stud muffin."

"Good morning, beautiful."

"You feel like some breakfast?"

"Yeah, that's cool."

We showered and dressed for the day. I prepared the scrambled eggs and bacon, while T.C. fixed the toast, coffee, and juice.

"You know, T.C., I don't take sex lightly."

"Yeah, Baby. I know."

"Well, I think we should go ahead and get back together. Be a couple, again."

"We can't do that, Carmen."

"Why not?"

After a long slow breath. He said, "Because I got married this weekend, to Carla. She's pregnant."

"What? You sorry son of a bitch. You got married and still came back and laid with me? I'm going to break your neck. You've been sniffing around me all these months talking about getting back together. I unknowingly committed adultery?"

Before realizing it. I had jumped up, ran across the table, and punched him in the face three times. I had become a mad woman. T.C.

was finally able to grab me from behind and pin my arms down.

"Carmen, I'm sorry. It was a shotgun wedding. Her brothers are ruthless and they threatened to harm my family. I love you, but what could I do?"

"You're always sorry for something, T.C. You could have kept your penis in your pants, you low life dog. Get the hell out. Get out. Get out. Slither on out of here like the snake that you are. I think I hear Satan calling you."

He let me go and I kept pushing him to the front door. However, before he made that final step across the threshold, I could not resist taking my foot and kicking him in his ass as hard as I could. Bull's eye. Right on the tailbone. He jumped and howled like a scalded cat.

"I hope you grow fungus and it falls off. You sorry, lying bastard. You're lucky I don't have a gun, because I wouldn't just talk about it, I'd do it. Damn."

What was anger, immediately took a downward spiral to sadness and despair. Ever sit by a window on a cold snowy winter day and see a baby bird fall from its nest, then feel an immense sorrow for that animal's doomed predicament? I felt that I was a total failure at relationships. Even when things appeared to be going well, it was really the opposite. I hated myself, and everyone around me. I wanted to kill myself.

Okay. I can make it. I can make it, I thought to myself, as I cleaned the kitchen. Then I went to my room, turned on the radio, and laid across the bed. It was an unseasonably cold sunny April day. Oh, no. Our song is playing. "Love Ballad," by LTD featuring Jeffrey Osborne. I began to cry uncontrollably.

Living was no longer enjoyable and relationships were taking too much effort for the little bit of happiness they gave in return. Every song drew me deeper and deeper into depression. I had earned my third load of bricks, and my wall was building. My life was in a total downward spiral. I reached over to the small gas heater that sat on the floor, next to my bed and turned it down until the flames disappeared. I tucked a towel under the doors and laid back on the bed. All I have to do now is close my eyes and go to sleep.

At that moment, the phone began to ring. Yet, I had no desire to answer. Whoever it was finally gave up. However, then it began to ring insistently, wrecking my silence.

"Hello."

"Carmen. Carmen. Why haven't you been answering the phone?"

"Ah, I-I was busy, Kathleen."

"You sound horrible. What's wrong?"

"Nothing. I have to go."

"I know you better than that. What's wrong?"

"T.C. and I are broken up for good. He got married this past weekend. But he didn't bother to tell me until after he spent the night."

"Oh, my God. Hang on, Carmen. We're coming to get you."

It seemed as though only seconds had passed when the Lufkin 6 showed up banging on the door. Upon entering, they busied themselves like a military team. One got my personal items out of the bathroom, two packed some clothes, another cut the gas all the way off, while the fifth opened some windows. Kathleen consoled me and helped me put on my coat.

"No man is worth killing yourself over. Besides, if you're dead, you won't be able to make him pay. You're staying with us for a while, Carmen. This isn't a time for you to be alone," Kathleen said.

Four of us piled into Kathleen's car, and two drove my car and we headed to Kathleen's apartment. It was an average three bedroom, two bath. The girls lived in the same complex. I slept in one of the twin beds in Regina's room. They took turns watching over me. Preparing meals, aiding in my showers, and doing my hair. Again, my heart had been broken, my innocence stolen, and my spirit scarred. There would be no going back.

Though not fully recovered, I was able to resume classes after a week. I walked the campus like a zombie. My love anthem changed from "Love Ballad" to "Holding On", by LTD featuring Jeffrey Osborne. It is hard to hang on when the love is gone. I sat on the brick wall in front of the student union, for a snack between classes. It seemed like more couples than usual holding hands as they passed. They appeared so happy. Clueless to the pain of love. I bit into my apple as hard as I could.

It was a slow Friday night on campus. No parties or concerts, and I had studied enough. The Lufkin 6, Kathleen, Regina, Wanda, Willete, Olivia, and Judy, wanted to play cards, but this time for small change. Firstly, we had to go to the grocery store for snacks and the other items necessary to mix drinks.

On the way back to their apartment, we encountered one of the girl's neighbors. I had seen this young woman before around campus, and in the apartment complex parking lot. She was always with some guy, smooching. They sucked face so much. I thought they would suffocate each other.

"Hi Janette. How's it going?"
"Just fine, Kathleen."

"Janette, I want you to meet a friend of mine. Her name is Carmen. Carmen, this is Janette. She lives next door."

"Hello, Janette. Nice to meet you," I said.

"Same here. Thanks for the light bulbs. I'll be sure to return some to you, Kat."

"Don't worry about it girl. Hey, we're having a party next weekend. Why don't you come."

"Cool. I'd love to come, Kat. Thanks for the invite. Bye."

"What party? I didn't know about a party," I said

"Oh, I just decided it was time for a party. It' will help with your mood, Carmen."

"Carmen, we're throwing a psychedelic party next Friday night. It's time to get you out of that funk girl. Two weeks is long enough to mope," said Regina. As she opened the door to help with groceries.

"I don't know about a party, Regina. I'm just not in the mood."

"That's the point, my Sistah. We need to get you in the mood, and what better way than to throw a party. Not another word from you, said Kathleen. We're going to start calling tomorrow. Tah-tah."

As we put the groceries up, and started to mix some drinks, Kathleen leaned over and whispered, "Janette lives next door with her boyfriend."

That was shocking news to me, because it was not a widely accepted lifestyle in those days. I would have never considered living with a man that was not my husband. He gets all the comforts of home, while you get to be his personal maid and humping bed. I wondered if her mother knew. I had to know more. Janette's open fornication intrigued me.

"So, what's the scoop on your neighbor?"

"Well, she moved in a few weeks after the semester started. She's a senior business major," said Kat.

"I don't remember her from any other parties," I said.

"That's because you had your own drama going on girl," said Regina.

"I have seen her on campus and around here. I've only seen the man around here, not campus. I don't recognize him from school."

Mystically, their behavior with one another captivated me. They engaged so easily, and seemed to be enthralled by the others touch, sight, smile, and smell. I wondered what their secret was for such a happy relationship. They had obviously been together for a long time.

"Word is he's married, and he only comes around when he can get away long enough from his wife. Rumor is he's paying for the apartment. She's his little cat on the side," said Kathleen.

"No! She's accepting trinkets for her virtue? Honey, doesn't she know that the wife gets the real cash, and the mistress gets the grass. The wife gets the name and benefits, while the trollop gets second place. She'll never be number one, and he'll never truly respect her! And if he does eventually make an honest woman of her, the only thing she can count on, is losing him by an affair with someone else," I said.

"I guess nobody told her that, Carmen. That's not all. You can hear them, sometimes, late at night. It's hard to make out what's being said. But, there's a lot of knocking, bumping, mumbling, and screaming. They are pretty animated, those two," said Wanda.

I wondered in silence about the life Janette was leading in the shadows. About the choices, she was making. What were her reasons for such a path? To some it is the hip and in thing to do. Nevertheless, not for me. I would just as soon be without a man than to knowingly be his concubine. I never contemplated the opportunity for a lifestyle like that.

Everything was set. We had chips and dips, peanuts, finger sandwiches, and drinks. We began our game of spades. Each time a team would lose, they would have to pay a quarter to the winning team. Moreover, an additional quarter for each book they did not make in their bid. Kathleen and I were kicking butt. Wanda and Regina were talking plenty of smack about their phantom comeback. Judy and Willette had next, while Olivia read a book.

During our game, we began to hear the bumping, knocking, mumbling, and low-pitched screaming that Kathleen had referenced to earlier that evening. The girls began to mock the sounds creeping through the wall. However, to me something was strange about those sounds, and I felt a deep concern crying from the recesses of my soul.

"There they go again," laughed Kat.

"She's going to need a back brace, if she keeps that up," smirked Regina.

"Some of us ain't that lucky," said Wanda.

"I think something is wrong. It doesn't sound normal to me," I said. "Maybe we should call the police."

"And tell them what, Carmen? Officer, get over here quick. My neighbor's man is screwing her brains out," said Wanda.

"Okay, then let's go over and check. We could ask them to keep it down," I said.

Suddenly, there was a tremendous banging on the door. So much so that I feared it would cave in. Kathleen jumped up to answer the door, and Janette came falling in. She was bloody and bruised. Her left eye is swollen, and her lips split.

"Please, help me. Please, please," begged Janette.

"Quick, Kat. Lock the door," I shouted.

It was too late. Janette's man kicked in the door, knocking Kat to the floor. He was brisk and brutal. Grabbing Janette by the hair, and slapping her. "Get your ass back home. I'm not through with you," he shouted.

"You bastard." I kicked him in the shin, shoved the palm of my right hand into his nose, elbowed him in the stomach, so he doubled over, and then kicked him in the head. He hit the floor hard.

"Damn, Ms. Bruce Lee. Where did you learn that?" said Regina.

"Two brothers, and a freshman self-defense class. Call the Police, and tell them we'll need an ambulance. Wanda, will you get a wash cloth for Janette, and make sure Kat's okay," I said.

Next weekend arrived in no time. The girls pulled together a decent party. The apartment was packed and was on the one. We gave the people small flashlights covered with various colors of paper at the end. It ripped with songs like, "Get the Funk out of my Face," by Brothers Johnson; "Tear the Roof of the Sucker" and "Flashlight," by Parliament;

"Brickhouse," by the Commodores; and "You & I," by Rick James. Ah-h-h, Yeah! The party was heating up. The girls were right. This party was going a long way to improving my mood. I was enjoying Beau's company, when a commotion was at the front door. It was T.C. and he was trying to get through to find me. Word had spread fast about what happened between us, and no one was empathetic with him.

"Carmen. Carmen. I need to talk to you!" T.C. shouted.

"Hey, man. You gotta get out of here with that mess. She doesn't want to talk to you." Beau said.

"Get outta my face man. I'm not talking to you."

"Punk, I'll knock you out. Carmen doesn't want to talk to you." Beau's football buddies were gathering around T.C., ready to pounce on him.

"All right, all right. Stop this male crap. T.C. you have two minutes." I said.

"Great. Let's go outside, Carmen."

"Oh, no. I'm not going outside with you. You have two minutes, in the bathroom, now."

As we entered the hall bathroom, Beau stood guard at the door.

"What is it, T.C.?"

"It's my brother, Donald. He's been shot."

"What? By who? When? Is he all right?"

"He'll live, Carmen. One of my brother-in-law's has shot my brother in the leg. I told her that I was still in love with you and I asked for an annulment. Her brothers retaliated."

"So, you decided to come crying to me? That shit is your fault. You should have never let her come sniffing around in the first place. You broke my heart and now you want to talk?"

"I needed someone to talk to, and I thought I could talk to you, Carmen."

"You thought wrong. Get the hell out of here."

"No. I love you. I need you."

"Let go of my arm and get out. You should have thought about that before you unzipped your pants and said I do."

Male testosterone had its way and Beau burst through the door.

"All right, man. Your time is up. Get to stepping."

"You need to mind your damn business and get out of my face, pretty boy. I know you want my girl."

"Look who's talking. Newsflash, Joker. She's not your girl anymore. Now, you better get out of here before this pretty boy kicks your ass. It's punks like you that make it bad for the rest of us guys." Fists started to fly and six of the football players ran in, grabbed T.C., and threw him out the front door.

"Are you all right, Carmen?"

"I'm fine, Beau. Thank you."

"You can thank me by dancing to this Marvin Gaye. Okay, everybody. Shows over. Let's party."

Janette had to spend a week in the hospital. Her bruises cleared up, but it would take a lot longer for the scars she incurred that night to dissipate. Janette pressed charges, and we all gave witness. Would you believe that fool's wife took him back?

I hardly knew Janette but, I curious about her plight. I had visited her twice during the week, and promised to take her home from the hospital. On Friday morning, she was to come home from the hospital, and I was there right on time to give her a ride. We sat and talked while the nurse got Janette's discharge papers together.

"What is it, Carmen?"

"Nothing. What do you mean, Janette?"

"You think I don't see how you look at me when you visit? You're wondering why I would allow some man to treat me the way Kyle treats me. But, you are just too polite to ask."

"Well, those thoughts have crossed my mind. Janette, you're a beautiful girl, and as far as I can tell, you're an excellent student. You have a bright future ahead of you. Why allow someone to bash your face in?"

"Huh. You know when I was a little girl, I saw my dad hit my mom. She would tell me that it was nothing. That he was stressed from work. We just needed to be a little more understanding, and pray for him. After all, he is the man of the household, and his job as the man was to provide us with housing, clothing, and food. I looked at her and said, "But what about love mommy." She said, oh yes, baby. He loves us very much."

The nurse came in to give Janette her instructions. I drove her home, gave her the pain medication, and tucked her into bed. I contemplated upon her revelation on my drive home.

MY SECRET ISLAND

I've taken my love to my secret island.
It's a place located somewhere deep inside of me
made from the remnants of shattered love affairs
And family anchored by insecurities

I call my island "Never More."
I know this is a strange name indeed.
But, as long as my love stays upon its barren shores,
Never more would another love find me.

Carmen

CHAPTER 16

In May of 1978, the spring semester was ending and I missed my girls. I managed to pull a despicable 2.9 GPA. This will wreck my chances for medical school. I decided to spend the summer in Houston, and take some extra transferable classes to boost it back up. Of course, I will have to do summer school next year, as well. I also acquired a part time job with a department store in the Galleria Mall. TheLetter, Bethany, and I continued to meet at least once a month in Houston for partying. It was doing all of us some good. Somehow, we kept each other grounded. I love them so much. Even with our disagreements, I would not trade their company for anything. I almost did not hear the phone ringing, with the music up so high.

"Hello, speak to me."

"Hi, Carmen. It's TheLetter. How are you?"

"Doing great."

"Really. I've been trying to reach you for a while now. Don't you ever check your messages?"

"Actually, I hadn't been back home until a few days ago. Things ended badly with T.C. and I. So, I spent some time with friends."

"Oh. Anything I can do?"

"Nope. It's been handled. But, you could get rid of that slime you call a boyfriend."

"Well, you don't pull punches do you? Damian and I aren't together anymore."

"What? You're kidding."

"No. It's true. I didn't see him for days. Then he showed up with almost all of the money I had given him. He looked bruised up, too. At first, I thought my brothers had something to do with it, because they showed up to visit for a few days and that's when Damian disappeared on me. Shortly, thereafter, he returned the money."

"There is a God."

"Whatever. I had to get an abortion. He would have nothing to do with me after I told him I was pregnant, and he didn't believe the baby was his. He said, if I had the baby, then he would make me take a paternity test to prove it."

"That dog knows you weren't sleeping with anyone else. He just wanted to mess with your mind, TheLetter. I knew that all along. Wow, a lot has happened since I saw you last month."

"Well, his method worked. I was in a mental hospital for three weeks and I've been seeing a psychiatrist twice a week."

"I'm sorry," I said. "What I know is that you've had enough disappointments to last a life time. What I'm sure of is that you should be looking for a man that is progressing, not digressing. That is positive, not negative. That lifts you up, not put you down. That is inspiring, not contriving. That is not rejecting of you, but accepting. Do you understand what I'm saying to you? All you need is to go shopping with your girls. I'm packing for the summer break now. Meet us Friday, two weeks from today, in Houston for shopping and partying. Okay?"

"All right, Ms. Jackson. But, how did you know about Damian? How could this have happened?"

"Do you ever investigate your own life, like you do for your clients? This is how it could happen. You take a very loving and compassionate person, who puts a roof over someone's head. Give them free rent, spending change, and voila! You have a leach."

"Funny. See you in two weeks, Carmen. I'll leave you a message at your uncle's with my flight information."

The days flew by; and, I indoctrinated into my new part-time summer job. I started in the games department. It was fun because I took the time to show customers how they worked. I called it, paid to play. One day a rather handsome looking Gentleman of Jewish heritage came in. He browsed around a bit and then left. I would see him every other day or so. Finally, he spoke and asked me some basic questions about a beautiful gold chess set.

"Hello. How are you today, Miss?"

"I'm wonderfully well. Thanks for asking. Can I assist you with anything?"

"Yes. My name is Bernie Shapiro. I was wondering are these pieces 24K gold? Is it an imported piece?

"Yes, it is."

"Chess, the game. Do you know it?"

"Well, a little. My brother plays."

"The queen. Such a strong and beautiful proud piece. An invaluable supporter of the king."

"I guess so. I never thought of it that way."

"It is true, my lady. Would you consider going out with me?"

"I don't even know you."

"Hence the reason for going out. To get to know one another, Carmen."

"How do you know my name?" He whimsically pointed at my nametag. "Oh."

"Well, will you give me the pleasure of your company? I promise you that I am a perfect gentleman."

"I really can't. I'm sorry."

"No need to be sorry. I'm probably rushing it a bit. Your beauty has enraptured me, and I couldn't help myself. Are you involved with someone?"

"No."

"Then, is it because we are of different backgrounds? I have no qualms about that, and you are of a proud and beautiful heritage."

"Thank you. We are all one race, the human race. I love all cultures, too. Let's be for real, man. People will stare and it will be hard for us. I'm just not ready for the stigma and glares that an interracial relationship would bring. Besides, I'm just not ready to be with another man at this time."

"Oh, I see. Pains of the past and skeletons in the closet. I won't push, but let me say this. I will treat you like the queen that you are."

"I have to get back to work. Take care, Mr. Shapiro."

Bernie Shapiro would come to the store regularly, within the next week, asking me to go out. He was a nice looking young man. He stood about five foot eleven, had thick curly dark brown hair, with ever so lightly golden blonde touches from exposure to the sun, and a pleasant smile. He was very intelligent and I enjoyed our detailed yet quick conversations. His family owned a jewelry store in the mall, and a restaurant. Bernie was completing his medical residency at the University of Texas Health Science Center. This was particularly interesting, since I was working on my

Bachelor of Science degree, and then planning to go to medical school myself.

I would always abruptly cut him off when he got too close. Not wanting to be close to, anyway. I had always wondered what it would be like to be with someone of a different race, but I just could not. He is one I eventually regretted letting get away.

The weekend was finally here. I picked up TheLetter at the airport Friday night, after work. I am so glad she had the finances to fly down and visit on a regular basis. We ordered pizza and cokes, and stayed up most of the night commiserating about our failed relationships and the pain of our abortions. Saturday morning we met Bethany at the Galleria Mall food court.

"Hey, Bethany. What's shaking?"

"Not much, Carmen. I missed you. Hi, TheLetter. How have you been?"

"Doing without, but it's got to get better."

"Well, pray. Pray real hard and maybe you'll get some tonight," said Bethany.

"That's quite all right. I am not desperate, and I don't sleep with a man after only knowing him for a few hours," gasped TheLetter."

"Hmm. Could have fooled me," said Bethany. Carmen, you're looking good girl. What's the taste D'jour?"

"I want to look really hot tonight. Something slinky, real fitted. You know?"

"Well, let's get started and do some damage ladies. I need some serious pumps because I am on the hunt!" Bethany said.

With that, we began our spree. Yakking and laughing all the way. There was so much to see, and the mall was full that day. Full of every type of man. We pointed out features that we liked or disliked about each. We even poked fun at the scantily dressed women, who had the nerve to wear tight, short outfits with a distasteful splendor. Where are the fashion police when you need them? Some of these people should get a ticket. My sisters, my sisters. Why do we think we need to exhibit our breasts and our asses to get a man? We let it all hang out, like an open book. We, as women, should follow a basic rule of etiquette. It should be short enough to be interesting, but long enough to cover the subject. One may not want the type of man one could catch dressed like that. You can bet his interest will not primarily be for your mind.

We ended up in a beautiful Italian shoe shop.

"Carmen, check out these black stiletto heels. You can be like Ms. Patti in these."

"TheLetter, please. I hadn't been able to wear six inch stiletto heels since 1974, '75 when I twisted my ankles in a pair of platforms. But, I tell you what. I wish I had beautiful Ms. Patti's blessed voice. Now, that would be something."

"I know that's right," said Beth. "LaBelle, now, those sisters can wear some heels. You think Prince's heels are as high?"

"Oh, no you didn't go there," said TheLetter.

"Oh-oh. Get back girls. These shoes are mine."

"What did you find, Carmen?" asked TheLetter.

"Look. A suede pair of multi-colored shoes, with a wedge heel, and front laces."

"My sister, my sister," sighed Bethany. "You are feeling mighty bold, aren't you?"

"Not really. I just feel happy. Why?"

"Girl. That shoe has gold, purple, and red. That is a bold shoe. It shouts, "I'm independent, and I don't care what anyone else thinks. No one will miss you in that shoe."

"Whatever, Beth. I see you found something. Simple black leather pump. Hmm. I'm sure you don't have a pair of those already." We smirked at each other and called the sales girl over to get our size. TheLetter was busy trying on shoes, right off the display.

"Miss. Can you bring me a size eight narrow," I said. Bethany asked for a size nine and a half.

"TheLetter, what are you doing?" I asked.

"Trying on shoes. What does it look like I'm doing?"

"Why are you trying on the ones off the display?"

"Because they fit and I don't have to waste time waiting for my size to be brought out."

"Also, because you are just a bit tacky," Beth snarled.

"Why does it have to be tacky, Bethany? Why is it that when something isn't the way you would do it, it's tacky or classless?"

"Because there is a certain etiquette in doing things. Something you obviously know nothing about, girl."

"I know a lot more than you think. You want me to show you some of it, you stuck up......"

I quickly interceded. "Ladies, ladies. Must you always go at it like this? Now, calm yourselves and let's enjoy our weekend. Agreed?"

"Talk to your girl with the shoe fetish, Carmen. I'm cool."

"I'm cool, as well," said Bethany.

I purchased the shoes and then shopped for the outfit. I found a deep purple jersey knit jumper. It had a rounded neck, but dipped down to my hips in the back. The sleeves were three quarter. It was a hot look, and felt cool. I also purchased a gold chain belt to go with it, and it picked up the gold in my shoes. Look out club. Here we come.

FOR I AM

I'm here to find if you want me,
But I'm just so very hard to keep.
I bring pleasure to those who do have me,
But when I'm lost, thus the sky do weep
I'm in the joyful smile of children,
In the thoughts of lovers embraced.
And in the peace you find within yourself,
When you put aside your life's mistakes.

I've been sought after through all the ages,
In every culture the world around,
And died many deaths in the darkness of life,
But in this light again I can be found.

Oh, I'm wanted for so many reasons,
Some good some bad you would deem.
For I am what is called "Happiness,"
desired by all, yes, by all indeed.

Carmen

CHAPTER 17

The hottest club in town was located in downtown Houston, called "The Hurricane." It was a three level building full of mirrored walls, disco balls, and colored lights. The levels were broken into different decorated sections. One area was a safari theme, another was like a fifties California soda shop, another area was like a jail, and yet another was someone's tastefully decorated living room. Each level had its own dance floor and the music beat throughout the club. A line of people waiting to get in was around the building.

We were all gussied up and ready to party. Bethany adorned in a royal-blue top with chiffon elephant legged pants. TheLetter wore black leather hot pants and a shear lace top, with a black vest that almost hit the floor. This surprised me, since she had been the most reserved of all of us. You never know how a failed relationship will change a person. I quickly parked the car in a lot a block away. We were not worried about getting in, because Bethany had connections. She always knew someone in a position of authority. She believed that was important to make it through life. We ran across the street, as the guys howled at us. I looked at my friends thinking to myself how lucky I was to have them. Upon our approach to the front door, the bouncer immediately lifted the rope. That was cool. We felt like stars.

"Hi, Bethany. You're looking great, as usual, girl." he said. "We reserved a table for you. Mary will show you the way. Have a good time, ladies."

"Thanks," I said. "He sure is a nice bouncer."

"He's the owner, not the bouncer, my dear," Bethany said. "I guess hanging out with Tony Simmons did provide me with advantages," Beth mused to herself as we entered the club.

We followed, Mary, the host. She showed us to a round bar height table midway in the club, and right by the dance floor. Perfect position. We could see the front door and the dance floor. We started our evening with stuffed mushrooms and shrimp cocktail appetizers. Then we ordered dinner. We liked to order different meals and then share. I got a lobster seafood platter with a baked potato-no butter, and a Caesar salad. TheLetter got the medium well T-Bone steak with fresh green beans, and steamed rice. Bethany ordered a large salad with chicken and shrimp pieces. That was no surprise, since she was always watching her weight.

The evening was moving on and the club was crowded. We sipped on our margaritas and strawberry daiquiris, as the music played. Guys had been coming by the table for the last hour, receiving one rejection after another. The poor souls got off lucky and they did not even know it. We could have slashed their throats. However, we still enjoyed looking at their hard bodies. That was as close as we were willing to get. After our recent break ups, we had gone through a short period of several meaningless dates. The guys that made it by the table that night were not the caliber.

First, there was Juan Carlos, the beautiful man who thought he was the Latino John Travolta. Then there was Earnel Roberts, the techno-weenie engineer who worked at the NASA space station outside of Houston. He was tall, too smart, and wore black rimmed glasses. However, he was so thin that he looked malnourished and he was boring. Oh, and there was Mr. Harvert, a gentleman that was twenty years our senior and looked at us like he was looking at a bucket of chicken. He promised to buy the person that dated him clothes and groceries. I guess that line worked for girls who never had much.

"Carmen, do you think we'll ever get married?" mused TheLetter.

"Why are you asking me that? Who cares at this point? Besides, you should be concentrating on your career, not some man," I said.

"You are the queen of sorrow, pain, and drama. Do you know that?"

"No, and I don't care. I may be the queen of sorrow and pain. But you my dear, without question, are the queen of drama"

"Carmen's right," said Bethany. "You should be concentrating on your career. But, if you get another man, then get a white man with money, TheLetter."

"Well, I think men of color are the best thing going. From the smooth light vanilla, all the way to the deep dark rocky road chocolate," said TheLetter.

"Yeah, right. And they usually end up being broke, or so cute that every other woman wants them," said Beth.

"Beth, do you honestly think that dating a white man, Italian, or Latino, means you won't have any problems? Girl you are dreaming," I said.

"What's up with men today anyway? Instead of taking the leadership role and being head of the household, they are holding on to a woman's coat tails and just working enough to get by. They make no long-term plans and follow no concrete steps in order to achieve them. At least, the one's we've met," said Beth.

"Oh, I don't know about that Beth. Sure there are a lot of bums out there, but there are brothers who are educated, with good careers, and who are true to their mates," said TheLetter. "We just haven't met any of them."

"Hey, Carmen. Whatever happened to that professional basketball player with the Houston Rockets that one of your rich classmates was going to introduce you to?"

"Beth, girl. We only had one date. He came up to the campus in his gleaming silver corvette, with sheepskin covered seats. A slamming stereo system that everyone heard a mile away. He was tall, good looking, and quite the gentleman. We danced the night away at one of the fraternity parties. T.C. was fuming. I just wasn't ready and his conversation was a bit boring. Aren't we here to party? Enough of this memory nightmare stuff." I said.

The music was loud and fast, my heart felt like it was going to beat right out of my chest. The dance floor was full, as the kaleidoscope colors spun across the walls. That is when I saw her. A tall slender beautiful goddess. She was all of six foot one, and her skin glowed even in the dark club. It looked silky smooth. Her eyes were large almonds and her lips were full, perfect, and moist. Her hair was dark, curly, and down to her mid-back. She wore a tastefully seductive gold sheer slinky dress that hugged every curve, with just enough gold sequins to cover her private areas. Her legs seemed to go on forever. All the men gawked and got a hard on, as she strolled from the front door, into the club.

"Who the heck is that?" smirked Bethany.

"I don't know. But, she's coming this way," said TheLetter.

"Carmen. Carmen. Close your mouth. You don't stare at people like that. C'mon, baby. Clean that dressing off your mouth," said Bethany.

"Hello, ladies. May I share your table?"

"Sure, no problem," I stammered.

"My name is Saree' Olayeni," she said, as she extended her hand and greeted each of us.

"My name is Carmen Robertson. This is Bethany Childs, and that is TheLetter DeLarue."

"So, is this your first time at the club, ladies?"

"Yes, it is. We've been to several in the Houston area. But, with limited leisure time, we're just getting to this one," I said.

"Actually, I've been here before and I know the owner," said Bethany. With an air of confidence and arrogance.

"Well, how proud you must be," said Saree'.

TheLetter laughed. She loved this war of words developing between Bethany and Saree'. "Are you from Houston, Saree'?"

"No, I am originally from Egypt. My father is a Nigerian engineer and my mother is from India. However, I currently live here in Houston."

"That explains your exotic look and accent. Just beautiful," I said.

"Thank you. You are so kind."

"Yeah, yeah. Whatever. So, what do you do for a living, Saree'? Hook for men in clubs," asked Bethany.

"I am a fashion model. Perhaps you've seen some of my work?"

"Oh, my goodness. Yes. I don't know why we didn't recognize you before," said TheLetter. "I've seen you in Ebony, Vogue, Glamour, and Mademoiselle to name a few.

"Yes, those were some of my jobs. What do you ladies do?"

"TheLetter is finishing law school, and working with a law firm in Minneapolis. However, Bethany and I are still in college. I plan to go on to medical school, and she wants to be an interior decorator," I said.

The emotions rushing through my body were so strange to me. Saree' had this piercing way of looking directly into the eyes of whom ever was speaking. A combination of weird and alluring.

"I take it, then, that no one is married?"

"No, Saree'," said Bethany.

"I would love to be married. But it just hasn't been in the cards," said TheLetter.

"Maybe if you stop being so easy, it would happen. No man marries a whore," said Bethany.

"You have a lot of nerve, Bethany. I am not a whore. At least when I'm with a man, it's for how he makes me feel, and not for his pocketbook," said TheLetter.

"Sweetheart. If you're going to give up the goods, you may as well get some lasting benefit for it."

"Now, who's the whore, Beth?"

"Saree'. I'm sorry. You have to excuse my friends. They tend to get a bit passionate about their personal views," I said.

"Oh, that's okay, Carmen. A cat fight is good for the soul from time to time. Would you like to dance?"

Bethany and Theletter's eyes almost popped out of their heads. I almost choked on the ice from my drink.

"Excuse me? I don't dance with other females. At least not in public," I said.

"What's the harm? There are so many people on the floor. You are here to have fun, right? Don't limit the possibilities."

"Okay. Sure, let's dance," I said.

Saree' and I went to the dance floor and had a wonderful time. Especially, when the oldies but goodies flashback songs came on. We imitated the different groups that the D.J. played. I have not laughed so hard nor felt so at ease in what seems like forever. TheLetter and Bethany stayed at the table monitoring our every move and turning down possible dance mates. I could feel their eyes burning a hole through me, like x-ray vision, when Saree' and I returned to the table, this time sitting next to each other, chatting and giggling the rest of the evening.

The car was quiet as we drove home. TheLetter did not say another word when we reached my uncle's home. She just said good night, and went to bed. The next morning Bethany called.

"Hello?"

"Hi, Carmen. You danced up a storm last night girl. So, how's your new friend?"

"Bethany. What is your problem?"

"I don't have a problem, but you might."

"Oh. And why is that?"

"Are you blind, C.C.? That woman was attracted to you. She probably wants to be your new best friend."

"Where do you get such crazy ideas, Bethany? How could you say that? Saree' did nothing to indicate that. Actually, I thought you, of all people, would appreciate her good manners, and stylish look. I do believe you're jealous. Don't be jealous, Beth. You know that I love you, and you're my best friend."

"I know that. And I'm not jealous."

"So, why did you call me at eight a.m.? Have you even been to bed?"

"Of course, I've been to bed. I just thought you guys might want to go to early Sunday services, Carmen."

"Um-hm. Why don't we do brunch? I have to get TheLetter to the airport at one p.m. You can go with me to drop her off, after we eat."

"Okay, C.C. That sounds good. I'll be ready."

The girls and I had a wonderful brunch. TheLetter had a trial she needed to help her firm prepare for, and she would not be able to come back to Texas until the end of August, depending on how things went. Bethany was going to New York for her internship. She landed a great opportunity to work with a famous fashion designer. She would also do several modeling gigs. We would all be too busy for our monthly rendezvous'. Saree' was leaving for a photo shoot in Canada, for a week. I decided to call her next weekend.

TODAY I THOUGHT OF YOU

Today I thought of you, this is honest and true
I prayed to the Lord with my heart, I thanked Him for you
God has blessed you with this life, many years He's seen you through
I often contemplate in my soul's color hue

What would my life had been like, if I never knew you
My guide bearer through turbulent times you've been
The summer, spring, winter, and fall
The sun, shades, rain, and wind

I miss your laughter, your touch, your smile
I'm sure you've known all the while
I miss the life that could have been, wondering if what happened was a sin
I see your face in the clouds, the rain, the sun, the moon
I thought of you today

Carmen

CHAPTER 18

In the following weeks Saree' and I became good friends. She was so easy to talk to, extremely gracious, and a lot of fun. When in town, she came to Huntsville to pick me up for a live weekend in Houston. Sometimes, Saree would stay in Huntsville and go to the skating rink with me.

We went to the rodeo one weekend, dressed in our jeans, boots, and hats. It was so much fun. We rode the carrousel, and when we were on top, we would throw popcorn over the side and laugh. Then we would play the basketball in the hoop game, and tried tossing a quarter on small plates. She was so cool. When we were not shopping, we would rent videos and eat junk food. She liked that, since she had such stringent guidelines as a model. We would take turns oiling each other's scalps and painting our toes and fingers. She also took me to a club called, "La Femme."

"La Femme," was a club decorated eccentrically and we had to go down stairs before entering the main club. I liked how glitter and balloons were always falling from the ceiling. The women there ranged from ugly to stunning, but they all were sheik. No one was dressed butch. No man in sight. Either this is a club for gay women only, or it's a support group for women that were hurt. Regardless, everyone was gracious and I always had a great time. We partied until five a.m. and then went to breakfast.

"Saree', you are just full of surprises."

"Well, I do like to impress."

"Anything else that I should know?"

"I enjoy a good time, wherever I might find it. I don't like to masquerade. If I did, then I would go to a masquerade party. I've had the benefit of an excellent academic education, traveled the world, and I still don't understand the mysteries of life. But, I'll tell you this, women should rule the world. That's it for now. Can't tell you too much, then there won't be any surprises."

"I see. Was that a gay only club, and are you gay?"

"Why? You aren't prejudice against gays, are you?"

"No, not at all. That's not what I was saying."

"Good, because I like all people, and I think you can have a good time just about anywhere. I just go where I feel comfortable, and where I can enjoy myself."

"You certainly know where the hot spots are, that's for sure," I said.

"That night you were with your friends. I saw you run from the parking lot, across the street, and into the club."

"Really? I don't know what to say."

"We're friends. Don't say anything, and don't stress anything."

We completed our meal and headed home to her luxury apartment. I loved my room there. I had my own private bath with marble floors. My bed had a goose down mattress and comforter. I had my own television and stereo system. It was great. However, millions of thoughts were running through my head. From being flattered to being repulsed. From happy, to angry, to confused. It was a lot to take in. I had never thought of that possibility in any serious manner. Forget it, is what I decided to do.

Normally, after such a late night I would sleep until past noon. I became so parched and I had forgotten to put a glass of iced water by the bed before retiring. I got up and wondered into the kitchen with my eyes closed. It was a familiar path. At seven a.m., the apartment was still pitch dark. Saree' had it prepared that way, so she could sleep in after a late shoot. I loved how she kept cold bottled water in the fridge. It tasted so great. I popped the cap and turned the bottle upside down into my mouth.

Those mixed drinks can really dehydrate a body.

"Can you pass me a bottle, please?"

"Saree'. Girl, you startled me. Here."

"Thank you."

"Where are your pajamas?"

"I don't wear pajamas, Carmen. I sleep in the buff. That's best for the skin because it allows it to breath."

"Well, Okay then. But you could at least where a robe when you leave your bedroom."

"Carmen, I'm usually the only one here. Unless my family visits. But, if it embarrasses you, then I'll use a robe in the future."

"That would be appreciated. Thank you."

We each said goodnight and went back to bed. I slept like a rock and awakened to the smell of bacon. My stomach began to growl. So, I took a shower and dressed for the day. It was two p.m., Sunday afternoon, and Saree' was preparing breakfast. She always ate breakfast first, no matter the time of day. But, she usually does not fix bacon.

"Good morning, sleepy head."

"Good morning, Saree'."

"I trust you slept well?"

"Yes, like a rock."

"Look, about last night. I didn't mean anything by it. I didn't even know you were up, until I came around the corner and saw the light from the fridge. I didn't think about going back to my room for a robe. I'm sorry."

"No. It's okay. This is your home and you have a right to be comfortable in it. Don't sweat it."

"Can I ask you a question?"

"Sure. Shoot."

"Do you have a nickname?"

"Yes. It's C.C. Given to me by a group of guys I used to go to school with."

"Hm-m-m. I like it."

"Do you have a nickname, Saree'?"

"No. I've always wanted one. No one's ever given me a nickname. I've tried myself, but it's never worked."

"Well, we'll just have to change that then, won't we? How about Shay? Shay Bella."

"Oh, Carmen. I like it. Thanks."

"No problem. Let's eat."

"Carmen, will you oil my scalp after breakfast?"

"Sure Shay."

Saree was naturally sensuous, and had subtle ways? The way she tossed her hair, flirtatiously. The way she gets so close to a person's face to speak. The way she threw her legs across my lap when we painted each other's toes. The way she laid her head on my thigh when I oiled her scalp and brushed her hair.

"Tell me a secret, Carmen? Something you've never told anyone," Saree asked?

"Hm-m-m. A secret unknown to someone else. Okay. I've often thought that I was forsaken by God to never be happy in a relationship. I've had absolutely no luck with men. But, I was also afraid that something was wrong with me. I don't know. You have beautiful hair Shay. I love to play in it. Your turn. Tell me a secret unbeknownst to anyone."

"I was raped at the age of twelve by one of my father's friends."

"Oh, my God. Saree', I'm so sorry."

"Mother was away when father's friend from Africa visited. They talked, laughed, smoked, and drank all day. I can still smell his fat sweaty body. Well, by night fall father had passed out. I was using the bathroom when the man walked in. It happened so fast and the floor was so cold and hard. I'll never forget the stone cold glare in his eyes as he stood in the doorway. It pierced through me like a knife. I haven't been right since. I hate men. But, I love you Carmen. My C.C. Bella."

"I love you, too, Shay. We've had some wild times girl. But, that was so long ago. You never told anyone or tried men?"

"Oh, sure. I've been through counseling. Father killed the man on one of his trips to

Africa on safari. Claimed it was an accident. I've dated. But, they either became physically abusive, or were to inpatient with me. Nothings helped. I still thought it was my fault, C.C."

"No way could anything like that be your fault. I'm glad you shared it with me, Shay."

"I don't sleep well. I've tried sleeping pills, and liquor. But I still awaken in a cold sweat. I get so tired. So, so tired."

How could anyone do something so ugly to someone so beautiful? This surprising disclosure explained why I hadn't seen any men with Saree', nor any pictures of men in her luxury apartment, other than her father and brother. I had my suspicions all along. Saree' and I had swapped repulsive secrets. She had bared all to me, and I could see straight through to her soul. I would not betray that all so treasured confidence that she had chosen to place in me. Now, not only did I have the burden of my pains, but I had her tragic revelation, as well. The same fowl act had occurred in both of our lives. A bond was been forged and we were now closer than ever before.

A different closeness than what I felt with Bethany and TheLetter. A strange warming, yet seductive closeness. I often spent the night in Saree's guest room. But not this night. This night was different. Saree' was hurting and I could hear her crying. She just needed someone to hold her.

"You're going to sleep tonight, Saree'. I'll stand watch. Just lay your head here, and don't worry about anything. Just sleep," I said.

I repeatedly and gently whisked my fingers through her hair and hummed a melody. She cried, and cried, and cried, until finally she fell into a deep slumber. We were kindred spirits. Kindred spirits that both had unrelenting demons in our closets that would not release our souls. No matter what we tried, we could not purge ourselves of these clanking bones that rattled endless pain and havoc in our lives.

"C.C. Bella. Good morning, sleepy head. Do you know you snore?"

"No. No one's ever said."

"Maybe you never slept so deeply before. I've made us breakfast."

"Oh, Saree'. How sweet. Thank you."

"No. Thank you. That's the first time that I've slept all night in years. I feel so refreshed. Thank you."

"You're so welcome."

We had breakfast in bed, and took a bubble bath. Splashing, giggling, and blowing bubbles. For the first time in what seemed like years, I felt relaxed without a care in the world, and happy. Saree' had this amazingly large sunken Jacuzzi marble tub in her bathroom. It was like a mini swimming pool. We were like a couple of five year olds, splashing water and blowing bubbles. Afterwards, we spent the afternoon shopping at the Galleria. Then we went to her high-class spa for pedicures, manicures, and massages. I was off from work, and skipped class that Monday to hang with my friend.

That evening we went to the nightclub. We loved turning men on just to turn them off. We would dance with each other so seductively. Twisting and touching. We used a routine that one of Saree's exotic stripper girlfriends showed us. By the time, we left the dance floor the men's trousers were standing at attention.

Being with Saree' was intensely fun, but I soon became deeply conflicted. What was brewing between us was too different from what my upbringing had taught me. I began to try to find answers to this dilemma in the Bible. Saree' planned to be out of the country on a photo shot for the next two weeks. That would give me time to think.

WHAT THE LORD HAS DONE FOR ME!

He's given me life, sight, taste, and smell
Now listen up, for this I can tell.
He's guided me through life's treacherous highway;
Give my God up! Oh Boy, no way.

He blessed me with great parents that cared and oh,
Of course, they taught us to share.
He's given me two precious children to raise;
For this, oh yes, I must give praise.
You ask, what my God has done for me?
I ask you this, what hasn't he given thee?

Carmen

CHAPTER 19

It was August of 1979. Our last year in college. Bethany was back from New York, with a promise of a job when she completed college. TheLetter was in her last year, and preparing for the bar.

It was a clear bright Saturday morning, and the temperature was a perfect seventy-two degrees. My uncle was up early, as usual, feeding his stock and preparing breakfast. I kissed him goodbye, with a promise to return shortly for breakfast. I was already packed and ready to drive back to campus. I decided to walk up that dirt road to see my great aunts first. They are long time soldiers. If anybody would know, these Ladies would. Aunt Hattie and Aunt Ida seemed to know everything about life and had so much wisdom. You could not pass through a room in their house without seeing a bible or a cross. I just hoped the questions I had would not upset them, or cause them to start trying to exercise some demon out of me.

There they were on the side of the house, at the old washtub doing laundry. Somehow, they never came up to the twentieth century. They still keep using that big old washtub and clothesline, with the wooden clothespins.

They are both very proud women and descendants of a strong lineage. All the siblings were tall, slender, and strong. Always singing "I'm a Christian Soldier." One would sing and the other would shout. They would go back and forth like that for hours. I had to wait for a calm moment between the two of them before I could make them aware of my presence. Finally, that moment came.

"Hi, Aunt Hattie. Hi, Aunt Ida. What's new?"

"Oh, My Lord. Our brother's grandbaby. Hey, baby. Give us some sugar. Now, which one are you?" They chimed in unison. Aunt Ida, and Aunt Hattie have been together so long, you would think they were twins. The way they would start and finish each other's sentences; or said the same thing, at the same time.

"I'm Carmen. Luke Robertson's oldest daughter."

"Oh, yes baby. Where is your momma?" said Aunt Ida.

"You know she's such a sweet kind woman, salt of the earth," said Aunt Hattie.

"She's at home in San Antonio. I'm going to college in Huntsville, now. I was hoping I could talk to you ladies about something very important."

As they stared curiously and intently at me, I laid the story out. It did not go well. They started crying out to the Lord, asking for strength, help, and guidance for this lost soul. Aunt Ida jetted into the house to get her Bible, and Aunt Hattie shouted, "Don't worry baby. We'll save you. We'll get that demon out for sure. He ain't gonna get one our babies. Oh, no he ain't. Where's some rope? Ida don't forget the candles and chicken foot."

The best thing I could do was to back out of there and run like the wind, back down that road. I grabbed my breakfast to go, quickly kissed my uncle goodbye, and drove off for school. I did not want them to catch up with me.

My school friends and I had initially joined a small local church under watch care. The bible study classes were to begin next week. I made a point to attend Sunday school, church, prayer meetings, and Bible study. All in an effort to find out if I would go to hell for what I was feeling.

Deacon Fatback and Sister Wetwash usually ran Bible study at the Greater New Light Baptist Church. A small old white wooden church a couple of miles from the campus. This church was over a hundred years old, and always reminded me of a time when blacks had only one church in the boondocks that they worshiped in. Their beliefs were just as old as the church. A time when the K.K.K. was outwardly pestering or killing any person that was different.

The fourth Wednesday, Deacon Fatback and Sister Wetwash spoke on Adam and Eve, and Sodom and Gomorrah. This was my chance to ask questions. I nervously raised my hand. I was glad the Lufkin 6 were there for services. We usually rode together.

"Yes, Sister Robertson?" Deacon Fatback asked.

"Ah, yes. If you love someone of the same sex, does that mean you're going to hell?"

"What do you mean, sister? Do you mean like you love your friends, your siblings, your parents?"

"No, sir. I mean like a mate."

"Then, yes Sister Robertson. One would surely go to hell," Deacon Fatback said.

"But, isn't God supposed to love everyone Deacon?"

Sister Wetwash was finally able to close her mouth. She quickly rushed over to my pew. "Now see her young lady. We'll have none of that talk in here. This is God's house. Now, you get on up and come out here to the vestibule."

"But, Sister Wetwash. Why? I was only asking a question," I said.

"Get up, now, missy."

I quickly rose to follow her out to the vestibule, and the Lufkin 6 fell in line. When I reached the vestibule, Sister Wetwash was pacing, with her hanky in one hand and flicking her nails with the other.

"Sister Wetwash. I didn't mean to offend anyone. I was just trying to get some answers."

"Well, you should know what is and is not appropriate to ask in the house of the Lord."

"If I can't ask these questions here, then where can I ask them? Aren't you supposed to help guide people?"

"You leave here and you leave here now. You are going to burn in hell for sure," she said.

I was humiliated, hurt, and there was nowhere else I could go. Why do people that claim to be Christian, often are the very ones who do unchristian like things? Kat and Regina put their arms around me.

"Carmen, we can help you. Come on. Let's go to our apartment and fix some hot cocoa." We dropped the other girls off, prepared some cocoa with cinnamon rolls, and sat at the kitchen table.

"Well, how is it you ladies can help me," I said.

"We don't claim to know it all. But, we did have an excellent pastor at our church back home, and questions were welcomed," said Kat.

"That's right," said Regina. "And how are you to know how to live your life, if you aren't taught? Carmen, we know you, and we know the hurts you've endured. You're still in pain, girl."

"Then tell me. Will I go to hell for being intimate with another woman?"

"Carmen. It is not for man to judge and say without reservation who is and who is not going to hell. That's God's job. But, it is written that he abhors the unclean," said Kat.

"Isn't He supposed to love me? Love everyone?" I asked.

"Yes, and He does. That is why He does not want your soul to be lost. He left guidelines for us to live by. But, man also has free will to choose," said Regina.

"Let's review some things that we already know. God made Adam, and then he made Eve, so, that man would not be alone. He told Noah to prepare for the flood. He told him to gather the animals, male and female, of each kind. For Noah's sons to bring their wives. In the marriage vows. Matthew 19:4-6, doesn't it say that a man shall leave his father and mother, and cleave to his wife?"

"Yes, Kat. I remember those," I said.

"The common thread here is that they all state a relationship of male and female. Not male and male, or female and female," said Regina.

"Now, let's dig a little deeper. However, understand this. We love you deeply and we know that you have been hurt unmercifully. That has a lot to do with your current dilemma," said Kat.

We spent the next six hours at that table reviewing the bible. We spoke on Genesis 18:20, and 19:4-6. The story on Sodom and Gomorrah. A city destroyed because of its great sin, and practice of sodomy. Then we went to Leviticus 20, which lays out statues for us to follow. Specifically, verse 13. "If a man also lie with mankind, as he lie with a woman, both of them have committed an abomination: they shall surely be put to death; their blood shall be upon them." Luke 17:34-36,....I tell you, in that night there shall be two men in one bed; the one shall be taken, and the other shall be left. Two women shall be grinding together; the one shall be taken, and the other left.

Romans 1:24-32, "God gave them up unto vile affections: for even their women did change the natural use into that which is against nature. And likewise men, leaving the natural use of the women, burned in their lust one toward another; men with men working that which is unseemly...."

"Carmen, the Lord is not speaking in a positive manner about such activities. We come to this world in sin. We must make a choice on how to live our lives. Will we keep living in sin? Or, will we resist temptation and live the Christian life that was intended for us? I'm going to love you, no matter what you choose, as I am supposed to do, said Kat. But, I have no heaven nor hell to put you in. If you have to choose, it is best to choose the guidelines laid out in the Bible, instead of what man on earth is doing at the time." They prayed together and then Carmen went home.

She did not necessarily agree with everything they said, but she appreciated their concern and effort. When she got home, she prepared for bed and then knelt down. She felt that she had been weak and confused. The Lord would not make her a certain way, and then blame her for it. Man has free will. She knew what she must do. Saree' and she both needed healing, and they could search for this together. She cried out to the Lord for strength to make it through this trail. Carmen had been so tired of intermittent sleepless nights. Of crying for seemingly unanswered prayers.

"Lord, Lord Jesus. I come again to you this night. Please, please, Lord I pray. Hear me.

Answer me. Forgive me for the death of an unborn child. I'm so sorry. Also, if you can, please do not hate me so much. Maybe one day I can learn to trust. Help me to help Saree'."

Just then, an overwhelming feeling came to me. Though I had my eyes closed, it became bright as daylight. I felt so loved; but, feared to open my eyes. Then a strong voice spoke to my heart and said, "I've already forgiven you. You just have to forgive yourself." I cried, but this time happily. It felt as a burden has lifted off me. The Lord fell upon my soul and spirit, like a spring rain. Quenching my thirst and giving my lost soul direction. His loving words rang so clearly. My tormented soul had been set free, and my famine was over.

That weekend, Saturday evening, I called Saree'. I missed her terribly and wanted to share the events of my recent enlightenment. However, it was not possible for us be a couple, ever. I really felt we should still be able to be dear friends. We talked for about thirty minutes about going to counseling together and starting the healing process. She had a hair appointment, and I had studies.

I called her again Wednesday evening to see about going to Houston for a weekend visit.

"Hello?"

"Hi, Saree'? This is Carmen.

"No, no. Not Saree'. This is Saree's Ma-Ma. Saree' is gone."

"Oh. Is she doing another photo shoot? When is she due back?"

"No, no. She dead. Saree' die last night," her mother said.

"What? How? Was it an accident?"

"She kill herself. I no talk no more. But, she left something for you. Services to be Saturday morning."

It was as if a truck had hit me. My beautiful Saree' gone. I could not believe it. Was this some sort of cruel joke? Why were these tragedy's happening? My heart was breaking again. I cried for the loss of a beautiful soul.

Thursday I skipped classes and called Bethany that evening. I laid the whole story out of all the recent events and about Saree's death. Bethany offered to pick me up from my uncle's on Saturday morning and attend the services with me. I really needed her support.

The services were somber, yet spiritually deepening. I was glad that Bethany attended the services with me. Saree' was gorgeous, even in death. I know she went to heaven. She was a wonderful person, who never hurt anyone. I do not remember her ever using a curse word, and she did not willingly fornicate. My life will never be the same.

It was a gorgeously ornate catholic church. The murals and statues were so angelic. One could not help but to get lost in their beauty. A young lady sung a solo. She was so petite, but had a mighty voice. The song, "If I can help somebody". I cried so much. Thank Goodness Beth was prepared with plenty of tissue. After the services, I extended my condolences to her parents. Saree's mother gave me a letter.

Dear Carmen,

If you're reading this letter, than that means I am no longer here to gaze upon your face. I feel like such a failure. I didn't want a man and I couldn't keep a good woman. I have no place on this earth where I fit in?
I loved you truly and deeply from the first moment I saw you. It was no accident that I asked to sit at your table. I'm sorry, if I confused you. That wasn't my intention. But, I find that I can't live with anymore sleepless nights, and the pain is unbearable. You are strong in your ways and beliefs, and I know you will be okay. I feel like I am an ugly beast from the pits of hell and that is where I shall return. Because, you see, suicide is the only sin for which, one can't ask forgiveness for.

I Love you my C.C. Bella.

Love Saree' (Shay)

My God. How could someone so beautiful feel ugly? You never know how a person sees themselves, or what torturous demons they have in their closets. The richest person could feel alone and unworthy. The most beautiful flower in the world could feel like a weed in a garden. Saree' will always have a place in my heart. She definitely was one of the beautiful flowers that has been plucked too soon.

CHAPTER 20

TheLetter made frequent trips back to Texas to cultivate our friendship. Of course, she had the means to do so. I had not flown to see her since I started college. Therefore, a trip was in order.

One thing I loved about Minneapolis was their change of seasons. Summer was summer, and winter was cold. It made it easier to get into the Christmas spirit. However, I could only stand it for a few days. Afterwards, I was ready to return to Texas.

Christmas break was coming, and this year I would spend a portion of it with TheLetter. I remembered the first trip I made back during the summer of my junior year in high school. It was great. At that time, Damian was not in her life and we had a ball. On that particular rendezvous, we went to Detroit to shop and party. My favorite was Greek Town. The flavor and culture were astounding, and the food mesmerizing. Because Missouri was closer traveling was more economical, which, was the only positive thing in that period of my life.

On another occasion, Bethany, TheLetter, and I had spent Thanksgiving weekend in

Chicago. No other family members, just us. We simply wanted to do something different. It was such a glorious time that we promised to meet in Chicago annually for a girl's weekend, once we had begun our careers.

Reservations for my trip to Minneapolis were completed, and excitement was high. I could hardly wait. TheLetter had promised to take me to the horse track, and a private gambling club. I had never been to a horse track, let alone bet on something. It made me feel grownup. Everything was so intriguing. I had dreams of grandeur. Dreams of becoming rich within a few hours. There was only one thing standing in my way. I did not know how to gamble.

The only thing I liked about flying was that it gets you there quickly. My flight landed on time and TheLetter was waiting for me as I had debarked.

"Hey, girl," TheLetter shouted.

"Are you talking to me, or someone across town?" I said, as I hugged her.

"I'm talking to you, of course, Silly."

"I was just checking."

"So, how was your flight, Carmen?"

"The usual. Too little space and a gabby neighbor."

"Well, I hope you at least got some sleep. Because our plans start this evening. But, first we'll go home. You can freshen up, and we'll get sharp as a tack."

"Looks to me like you need some rest, TheLetter. Why are you so pale?"

"Oh, I'm fine. I've just been working a lot lately."

"A lot of people work extra hours, but they don't go around looking anemic. Why is it that when you look this way, it's because of work?"

"Carmen, you are too suspicious. I am fine, okay?"

I was anticipating seeing her new home. She was such an industrious and ambitious person. She was always progressing toward the positive, at least, career wise.

Her home was in a nice middle class area of town. A grey brick façade, double car garage, and an abundance of trees and bushes. TheLetter hit the button above her visor, and we pulled right into the garage. When the garage door closed behind us, the kitchen door opened simultaneously. Initially, I thought it was some neat electronic trick, until the form of a man appeared.

"Who is that?" I gasped.

"Oh, that's Richard. Didn't I tell you about him?"

"No, TheLetter. You didn't tell me one mumbling word. Now, why is that?"

"I guess it slipped my mind."

"Yeah, right. Well, is he just going to stand there like that, or is he going to make himself useful, by getting the luggage?"

"Don't worry, Carmen. I got it." TheLetter gets out of the car and says, "Hi, Honey, we're back. This is my girlfriend, Carmen. Carmen, this is Richard."

"Hi, Richard. Nice to meet you."

"The pleasures all mine, baby."

"Maybe, you didn't hear her, Richard. The name is Carmen," I said.

"Yeah, right. Look here, baby. I need the car to run up here for some cigarettes. I'll be right back."

"Richard, I have plans tonight, said TheLetter."

"I'll be right back. Besides you had the car all day at that clinic."

"All right, baby. Just hurry back, okay?"

"TheLetter, what is he talking about?"

"Nothing, Carmen. I just went for a checkup that's all."

Four hours passed. We had bathed, dressed, had a bite to eat, and were in the middle of a game of gin rummy, when we heard the garage door go up.

"Who does that fool think he is taking your car like that?" I snarled.

"It's okay, Carmen. Sometimes, he just loses track of time."

"Why are all your boyfriends light-skinned with green eyes? Does that make you feel better about your own complexion to be with a light-skinned brother?"

"No, of course not. I just seem to attract that type?"

"Yeah, right. Forgot about that garbage you were spilling back in high school, huh?"

"I don't know what you're talking about. I love our brothers. All colors."

"But, you mysteriously only have the cuties as boyfriends, and you jump through hoops to keep them."

Richard wobbled in, kissed TheLetter, and belched. "I'm going to bed, baby. See you in the morning," he said.

"TheLetter, he lives here, too? Why did you let this man move in here? I only saw one car in the garage."

"He needed a place to stay. There were some maintenance problems at his apartment, and….."

"Yeah, he probably wasn't paying rent."

"No. They weren't making repairs and he refused to put up with it anymore."

"So, how was that your problem?"

"I have two extra bedrooms, Carmen. It's no big deal."

"First of all, he went into your bedroom, not a guest room. How long have you known this man? And is he paying any rent?"

"I've known him a month. And no, he's not paying rent. He's having a difficult time right now. Besides, it's just temporary."

"Must you fall for every cookie that comes out of the cookie jar? It's not temporary. He's your new best leach. And a month is not long enough before moving someone into your bed."

"You see. That's why I didn't tell you. You always blow things out of proportion."

"He's an inconsiderate drunk. He knew I was here to party with you, but he took the car anyway."

"I think I've had enough. Goodnight. I'll see you in the morning," She said as she threw the cards at me.

"No, you need to tell these men that you've had enough. Stop giving all of yourself up for free."

"Carmen, I said I've had enough. We'll discuss this tomorrow."

"No. We'll discuss it, now. How many times are you going to mutilate yourself? How many times will you return to that shabby little building in the shady part of town?"

"You don't understand. He loves me. He just isn't ready for kids right now."

"If he loved you, you would not have been at that clinic alone. If he loved you, he would use protection. Damn, if he doesn't want kids, then he should get a vasectomy. Why are you taking all the risks?"

"Goodnight, Carmen." TheLetter stormed out of the room and slammed her bedroom door.

My first evening, and we fought over some inebriated fool. It was supposed to be a time of sharing and bonding for us. Instead, it was a period of division and friction. Everywhere we went, he went. Everything that needed to be paid, TheLetter handled. This infuriated me.

I made a conscious decision to distant myself from TheLetter. I could not stand to see her avail herself to one unworthy bum, after another. Drama I did not want to watch; I was no longer going to make phone calls or write letters. Any contact would be from her.

It took two months for me to cool off. When TheLetter called, I would talk to her. However, I made no comments or inquiries into her personal life. The calls were pleasant, cordial, and to the point. Without any real depth. TheLetter was on the fast track with her career. Nevertheless, she was short on common sense. Like my Grandmamma Nan used to say, "You can have all the book sense in the world, but without common sense and wisdom, it don't amount to a hill of beans." TheLetter eventually kicked Richard out after hearing an intimate message on the answering machine, from his boyfriend, Andre. At least, that was the last I heard about him. Until Keon was born.

WHAT GOD HAS MEANT TO ME

I wondered who with love I could need
While looking across the large vast sea.
With a wounded heart and a bruised ego,
I wondered, Lord, O' where should I go.

My crowded heart,
the darkness of my mind,
you saved me Lord in the nick of time.
I've shed tears,
I've felt confused,
Only you, O' Lord, would not abuse.

Without you God, I could not see.
You put me down on bended knees.
I wondered, Lord, who I would need.
It's you O' Lord, the one I seek.

Carmen

CHAPTER 21

During this time, January 1980, Bethany had become a busy beaver. Her skills had to be exceptional. The college was preparing for their spring extravaganza, and they asked Bethany to lead the design and decoration of the set. She had a unique flare, and an eye for color.

The show would consist of a Greek beauty contest, with solos, a small skit, and a dance routine. Bethany was frantic that the March 1980 date would roll around before she was prepared. Thank Goodness the fashion/interior design department was helping. For Beth everything had to be just so. This anal behavior, sometimes, made her difficult to work with. However, no one could deny the outstanding results.

We spoke frequently, often until the wee hours, bouncing ideas off each other. Though my major was science, I loved the arts, and had a natural proclivity for sketching and painting.

Bethany had received the package I sent which included some possible themes, and several sketches. She called late one evening to review them with me. There had been a full day of auditions, and material purchases, as well as, setting up a celebrity guest appearance.

"Hi, C.C. I received your sketches. They're good, girl."

"Thank you, Beth. How are you doing?"

"Okay, I guess. Just a bit pooped. I'm eating a fast hot dog with chips, now."

"You're eating hot dogs? I've never known you to eat food like that before. You must be tired."

"Yes, I am. And I'm going to bed right after we finish."

"So, which one do you like, Beth?"

"They're all great, but, I'm leaning towards the one with the alternating black and red satin drapes that gather on the floor, with the nicely placed bold white Greek statues. I can't help looking at it."

"Great! Glad I could help. The theme for that one is, "Nothing but the Greek in Me."

"Carmen, can I call you back?"

"Sure. Is something wrong?"

"My stomach is a little upset. I think I'm getting heartburn. I'll call you back in about an hour."

"Okay, Beth. I'll be waiting."

I occupied myself in preparation for the next day. After class tomorrow morning, I would need to go put down a deposit on my graduation package. Cap and gown, invitations, memory book, and a ring. An hour had passed without a call from Beth. Once I showered and rolled my hair, two hours had passed. Now, I was concerned.

It was not like Beth to be late. I tried calling her for forty-five minutes, but the line was busy. Panic took over. The operator checked the line, but said no one was talking on it. Not knowing what else to do, I called 911 emergency services, and told them that I suspected my friend might have had a heart attack. That is the draw back from living off campus in your own apartment, no dorm mother to call.

The Prairie View emergency services had an immediate response. However, I thank them for not sending a bill. Not only did the paramedics respond, but the police and the fire department did, as well. The lead officer banged repeatedly on Beth's door until she finally stumbled forth.

"Ms. Childs, are you all right. Ms. Childs, we need you to come to the door," said the lead officer.

Beth was confused, and afraid to open the door. "Who is it?"

"The police. We had a call that you may be ill. Are you all right?"

"Yes."

"Can you open the door? We need to see you."

"Hold your badge up to the peep hole," Beth said. The officer complied. "All right. What is this about?"

"Do you know a Miss. Robertson?"

"Yes. She's my friend."

"Well, she was quite upset. Said you complained of some mild chest pain earlier this evening."

"Oh. Yes, I had indigestion. Heartburn you know. I ate hotdogs earlier, and they didn't agree with me."

"I see. Well, why is your line busy? Ms. Robertson tried to call, and the operator did not detect any conversation?"

"I guess I fell asleep, officer. The phone must not be on the hook good. I'll take care of it."

"So, you're okay, and you just had gas?"

"She just had gas?" chimed the second officer. "It's okay, everyone. Back it out. She just had gas. By this time, the complex neighbors had gathered to see what all the commotion was. The word "gas" repeated itself through the crowd. She just has gas. She has gas. It's gas. Gas."

My phone rung at one a.m. It was Bethany.

"C.C., have you lost your mind?"

"Girl, what are you talking about? I was scared for you."

"Well, I can appreciate that. But, I was so embarrassed. The police came, the paramedics, and a fire truck. Not to mention the large crowd that gathered. I would have made some money, if I sold tickets."

"Oh, Beth. I am sorry. They were just trying to do their job. Not embarrass you."

"No, that was over kill. The only reason all of those services came out here, was because they had nothing else to do. The police were banging on my door like it was a raid or something. Then they broadcasted the status of my bowels to the whole community. I'm not going to be able to show my face around here for a while. I'll have to wear a hat and sunshades."

"Beth, that is too funny. Oh my goodness."

"Yeah, yeah. Laugh it up. Get it out of your system, then I don't want to hear about it again."

"Oh, please. Why are you being so sensitive? If the shoe were on the other foot, you know you would laugh."

"Um-hm. So, how's TheLetter?"

"Fine, I guess. I haven't spoken with her since New Year's. Anyway, what are you doing calling me after ten p.m.? Disturbing my rest. Didn't your mama teach you that it's rude to call people past ten?"

"You woke me up. Sending your friends in blue over here to bang holes in my door."

"I love you, Beth."

"I love you, C.C."

"Good night."

"Good night."

<u>WHAT HAS HE DONE FOR ME?</u>

He's given me life, sight, taste, and smell
Now, listen up for this I can tell.
He's guided me through life's treacherous highway,
Give him up! Oh, boy. No way.

Blessed with great parents that cared,
And oh, of course, they taught us to share.
I have two precious children to raise,
For this, oh yes, I must give praise.

You ask what my God has done for me?
I ask you this. What hasn't He given thee?

Carmen

THE STRESSORS OF LIFE ARE IMMEASURABLE, BUT A PERSON KNOWS THEY'RE IN A STRUGGLE

CHAPTER 22

Bethany and I graduated May of 1980. TheLetter, had already graduated law school and passing the bar was not a problem. We could not attend each other's ceremonies, because they fell on the same weekend. However, we were together in spirit. Many years and additional trials would befall us, but that is another story in itself. The years and turbulence rolled by, finally bringing us to this pivotal twenty-year, high-school reunion in June of 1995.

Tonight was a night of reconnection. Bethany, TheLetter, and I had spent that Saturday together shopping for shoes. We dropped TheLetter off first. Bethany then asked Liz and me to wait, as she called out to TheLetter.

"Wait up, I need to speak with you," Beth said.

Beth ran up to the porch to speak privately with her. I do not know what she said, but they hugged and pecked each other on the cheeks. Bethany then returned to the car smiling.

"What was that about," I asked.

"Oh, nothing. Just setting things straight," Beth smiled.

"See ya later on tonight," TheLetter yelled as she entered the foyer of her parents' home.

"Beth, are you okay? What is she talking about?"

"Yes, Carmen. I asked her to meet us this evening at my parents' house before we leave for the reunion. You know, even though she is not in our class, I feel that she is as much a part of this reunion as anyone else. So, I figured that it would be nice to have photos of us all dressed to the nines, as we prepare to wow the men who will secretly whisper to themselves, "If I had only known then, what I know now!" as they see us enter that ballroom. I cannot wait to see the heads turn, along with the stomachs. Oh, and the stomachs will turn. You know I saw Joe Lincoln as we were leaving the shoe store. Remember him?"

"Fine-ass Joe "Shoes" Lincoln? The Star of the football team? Hell yeah, why didn't you say something, Beth."

"Well, Carmen, like granny said, "'If you can't say anything nice, don't say anything at all.' After seeing Joe's spare tire, or should I say set of four tires around his midsection, I thought I would save you the horror. So, like I said, I know some stomachs will be turning tonight. Literally and figuratively, if Joe's physic is any indication of what's to come."

"Bethany, you are simply scandalous."

"Aren't I? And you know that you love it. But really, Carmen, TheLetter has been through a lot. Hell, we all have. Being at home makes me realize that no matter what the chaos love can conquer all. I mean just look at them. Back together, AGAIN!!! Now, if that can happen, surely TheLetter and I can finally bury the hatchet and begin to act as the mature, professional, up and coming sisters that we are, right?"

"Girl, I am so proud of you." We exchanged hugs.

"It is our reunion year, and it is time to start living," said Bethany.

She may not have wanted to admit it, but she had always loved TheLetter. Even though they fought like cats and dogs. That was just their way. Too bad, it took them twenty years to come to terms with the type of relationship they had. Better late than never, I supposed.

We all met at Beth's' parents' house around six in the evening. I introduced Albert to Bethany and Chad. TheLetter and her younger sister arrived shortly after for pictures. They looked like Essence magazine cover girls. TheLetter's petite frame sported a one shoulder white beaded cropped top, complimented with palazzo pants in black satin with a sheer georgette overlay. Of course, those little feet sported the cutest pair of sequined evening shoes. Her sister, Crystal, wore an outfit that was almost the complete opposite, a black one shoulder top with white pants and sequined shoes from our mall shopping trip. They were enough to make any man who had not fantasized about ménage a trois; or, to consider one. I wore my new red spandex dress and sling backed red pumps. Bethany was in a beautiful black sequined dress.

I introduced the cover girls to my date, Albert. "Albert, this is TheLetter, and her sister, Crystal," I said.

"Well, well, well, I finally get to meet the infamous gang. TheLetter Delarue, what a sensuous name. One most befitting a sensuous young lady. It's my pleasure," Albert said. He was always trying to impress.

"Anyway, TheLetter, where are you and Crystal headed?" Bethany interjected sensing my displeasure with Albert's forward comment.

"Oh, we are headed downtown to the new club on the Riverwalk, The Crossroads. However, we'll follow you all downtown. Do a little meet and greet of old friends in the lobby; then, we will walk over from "I heard Liz mention that club. I hear it is where anybody who is anybody, and everybody with nobody goes," Beth joked.

239

"Yeah, the freaks do come out at night, you know? So, we will be there front and center to bear witness."

"Just make sure you call us with the 411 tomorrow on the freak sightings, cause I know with a full moon, they will be out in droves," said Beth.

"Ladies, I hate to interrupt," Chad said in his best attempt of a serious tone. "But, the reunion is at the Marriott, not here. So, we need to get a move on. Let's get these pictures taken and jet on down to the hotel, so I can get my grub, I mean groove, on."

Everyone laughed and the cameras and posing went on, nonstop for fifteen minutes. When the flashing stopped, it was hugs and kisses all around. It felt so good for the first time, it seemed that we, Beth, TheLetter, and myself, were on the same page, finally.

The reunion party was in downtown San Antonio, Texas, at the Marriott Riverwalk Hotel. This hip new club, TheLetter and Crystal headed to, happened to be just a mile away, on the opposite side of the Riverwalk.

The night was full of promise. White linen tablecloths covered the ballroom tables, crystal goblets, and china. The room was buzzing with the chatter of people reacquainting. Where have you been? What have you been doing? You are looking good. Due to all the camera flashes, you would have thought celebrities were there. Some people I recognized, and others I did not. There were a couple of speakers, who were our past teachers. A photographer herded the class over to the raised stands, and took a group photo. Then, we began dinner. Chicken breast with sauce, a baked potato, dinner roll, salad, and ice tea. It was not an exotic meal, but it got the job done. The meal was not the focus of the evening anyway. Beth and I sat next to each other and continued to chat until a gentleman approached our table and began to snap several pictures.

It was Leon with that big smile of his. He was sharp that night. Dressed in a green double-breasted suit, with a white banned collared shirt. Our school colors. He still had that high school physique that he had when he was the quarterback for the school's football team. However, I thought he was in TheLetter's class.

"Hi ladies. You look great," he said. Leon went around the table shaking hands with the men, and giving hugs and kisses to the women. Then he leaned over and whispered in my ear.

"I need to speak with you later. Okay?"

"Yeah, all right. I'll catch you at the after party, and stop taking pictures. My date might get suspicious," I said.

He snapped a couple more pictures and then made his way around the room. The evening progressed and for one night, I was able to forget my worries. The Mustang Lounge was the location for the after party. Not my usual taste. However, everyone in attendance had graduated from Sam Houston High School. The crowd hustled, bumped, and two stepped the night away. My date did not want to dance. Eventually, I went my own way. Leon asked me to dance, and I agreed. Turns out he lives in Atlanta, Georgia, and attends the same church as I do. I never noticed him before, but the congregation is over five thousand people, and we have three services on Sunday to accommodate the membership.

Unfortunately, Leon messed up when he asked me for my phone number and a date. I explained to him that I do not date, except to have an escort for a special event. I also do not care to be bothered.

"It was nice seeing you again, Leon. Take care of yourself, and goodnight."

I returned to my table, said my goodbyes, then my escort and I left.

"What was that about," my date asked.

"Excuse me?"

"That guy that kept taking pictures of you, and then asking you to dance?"

"Oh, of course, that's a classmate. But we've never been involved, if that's what you mean?"

"You could have fooled me. He was sniffing behind you all night. I don't appreciate some fool pushing up on my woman."

"Ah, newsflash. I am not your woman. I belong to no man, and you are just someone I spend time with when I feel the need."

"What? I thought we were getting along fine?"

"Right. We get along fine, as long as you stick to the guidelines that I laid out in the beginning. Now, if you feel you can't handle that, then you know what you can do. Besides, just because I date you, or even if I were committed to you, it doesn't mean that I can't speak to someone of the opposite sex."

"All right girl, all right. I was just hoping we could spend a little more quality time together. You've been so wrapped up with your little girlfriends lately. I mean what's that about?"

'First of all, it's not all right. We said that we were dating. Why can't we just do that? Date and have fun. Why does it have to culminate in some sort of committed relationship or marriage? The time I spend with my friends is my business. I have known them a lot longer than I've known you, and I haven't seen them in a while. So, excuse me, if I don't give you special attention during this weekend. Look, all I'm saying is that two people should discuss whether they're going to the next step in a relationship or not. You can't say you're okay with just dating, and then independently assume something else. And I don't think that because you're dating someone, it means you need to have sex. If I cocked my legs open for every man that I had three to ten dates with, then I would have a lot of notches on my bedpost. A few dates and meals does not earn you the panties. That I'll save for marriage,' I said.

"Don't get so upset girl. Ain't nothing wrong with two people that care about each other having sex. And you don't know, we could have ended up married. You know I'm crazy about you. I would do anything to be with you."

I remained silent until we pulled into my parent's driveway. "I know that that is no type of guarantee, and I'm not laying with you in the hopes of a wedding ring. So, you can stick it in your ear. If you care about me, then you'll care enough to get to know me, and to marry me when and if it's right," I said.

"You know, Carmen, you are starting to push up on forty and the ratio of eligible black men in particular, to women is like one to one hundred, you know. So, you need to get off your high horse and get real about what you want."

"That's it. You need to leave. I think this conversation is over. You…."

"Oh, no. It ain't over until I say it's over, Carmen. You see, that's your problem Miss I don't need a man, Carmen. All that independent bullshit! You need to back down and quit acting like you're Virgin Mary. If I didn't know where babies came from, well, let's just say you didn't get those crumb snatchers by yourself."

"I'm only going to ask you once to leave, Albert. Now, I'm telling you."

"You ain't telling me shit. I didn't take my weekend off from the base to be played like a fool in front of your friends. Now, I'm leaving, since you're calling it a night so early, Carmen. I'm going back downtown to party. Maybe the women down there can appreciate a man, and know what to do with one."

"It's your world, Albert."

You could only hear the frogs and crickets as we walked to the front door. I gave him a peck goodnight and then closed the front door.

I am not sure how long he stood on the porch, nor did I care. Nevertheless, I went to bed.

Albert gets on my nerves sometimes. I am sick and tired of his black mood that comes and goes like the wind. In addition, he never hesitates to talk about his military escapades. He loved that lifestyle and the horrible things he and his soldier friends did to the locals in Saudi, and other assignments. He was becoming too clingy, and calling too much.

The twenty-year reunion had been successful, and made for a wonderful weekend. That is until the call came. I had slept well, and as usual, the children were already up watching television. My parents were preparing for church services, which I had decided to pass on. The reunion picnic was at the park later that afternoon. The telephone had rang, and mother hurriedly answered it.

"Carmen, dear. Telephone. It's Mrs. De'Larue," Mother said.

"Hello, this is Carmen."

The last thing I remembered was the room went black. When I awoke, I felt like an alcoholic after a nights binge. I was weak and woozy. Mother, Bethany, Liz, and Daddy were all in my room.

"Momma. She's waking up," said Liz.

"Hi, sugar. How do you feel?"

"Like somebody hit me in the head. Where am I, Momma?"

"You're in the hospital. You've been here for two weeks. Liz, call the nurse."

"Hi, baby girl. You had us worried for a while there," said Daddy.

"Hi, daddy. Hey, Beth."

"Hey, sweetie. I thought I was going to lose you, too," Beth said.

"Lose me? What do you mean? Wait a minute, Oh, no. TheLetter! TheLetter's dead, isn't she?"

"Calm down, sugar. Don't make yourself sick all over again," Momma said.

"I remember. I remember Momma DeLarue called. She said TheLetter died last night. What happened," I asked?

"She and her sister went to that popular night club downtown, remember?" Beth said. "You know the one on the Riverwalk, called the Crossroads? Well, her sister, Crystal, said they were walking back to their car in a parking garage not far from the club. A man tried to rob them. He punched Crystal in the back of the head, and kidnapped TheLetter. Her body was found in an abandoned lot. TheLetter had been beaten and raped. The coroner's report, however, showed that no semen was found, and she was pregnant."

San Antonio was not a violent city. The most I have ever seen when downtown, at night, was a drunk regurgitating on the sidewalk. Nothing you would see on crime story. I still did not understand this crime. It was so brutal and isolated. Something about this did not set right with me.

"No, no. Not sweet TheLetter. Oh no. No."

My mother looked at Bethany angrily because she had told me the truth. However, Bethany knew that I had to know. The nurse came in with a sedative that she added to my IV. I could feel it starting to take effect. "When is the funeral? I have to go to the funeral?"

"Sugar, it was a few days ago. You've been in a coma for almost two weeks. They couldn't wait, not knowing when you would come around," Momma said.

"Why does God hate me Momma? Why?" I asked.

"You hush, now. God does not hate you, baby. Get some rest. We'll be right here with you. Don't worry," Momma said.

"Don't make promises you can't keep," I whispered.

After another week of tests and observation, I discharged from the hospital. My family hovered around me, afraid that I was so fragile

I might break. Bethany came to visit regularly, ignoring her businesses. The class reunion was June of 1995. It was now mid-July. I had not left the house, did not return phone calls, did not read the mail that was forwarded, and had no desire to do anything. My parents were becoming concerned.

"Sugar, you need to get out. You need to go back to work in Atlanta, and get the kids ready for school," Momma said.

"I don't want to go anywhere. My partners can handle the office, and the kids can miss a couple of weeks of school, if necessary. They're smart," I said.

"Carmen, I'm shocked at you," My mother said while sitting on the bed. "They've never missed school. What kind of example are you showing them? Baby, I know you're hurting, but, you can't give up on life. Trust me there is a gift in life for you," As she began to stroke my hair.

"Momma, I love you. But, can you please leave me alone?" My mother quickly rose.

"Fine, Bethany is here to see you. I'll check on you later. Come on in Bethany."

"Hi C.C. How are you?"

"I don't know Beth. I really don't know."

"Carmen, I know how you feel. But, you can't stay here and shut yourself off from the world."

"You don't know how I feel, Beth. All you ever did was quarrel with TheLetter."

"I loved TheLetter, too. I made sure she knew that after we dropped her off from shoe shopping. Confrontation was our way. I loved her, too. I also love you. Our trilogy has been broken. But don't you leave me by myself, C.C. Do you hear me? Don't you leave me alone."

"I don't know what to do, Beth. I feel like I died, too. It was happening all over again. There's nothing but blackness inside. A dark void from which I can't escape. Everything that I've loved has either died, or hurt me. I have nothing left."

"You have your children, Carmen. They need you, and they look to you for direction. What's going to happen to them, if they lose their mother? You also have you parents, and your sister. Please don't give up."

"But, I just feel so tired. So, so tired. Life is just too hard."

All I could do was cry in Beth's arms. She showed me TheLetter's funeral program.

"Carmen, I saw TheLetter's man."

"Who? Where?"

"At TheLetter's funeral. I think they said his name was Richard. He was crying big crocodile tears, slobbering, and yelling for her not to leave him. That he will be sure to take care of their son, little Keon. Girl, I didn't know he and TheLetter were that close in their relationship."

"What, Is that fool crazy? They weren't close. I didn't know he was still hanging around. He can't have Keon, anyway. TheLetter's will names me as executor of her estate, and the legal guardian of her son."

"Well, evidently, Richard doesn't know that," Beth said.

"I have to get Keon. We need to go to Minneapolis for the reading of the will, Beth." This was just the kick in the pants I needed. A cause, a piece of TheLetter.

"When is the reading of the will?"

"I'll have to get in touch with the attorneys office. There's probably mail at home about it already. Will you go with me? I have the key to her safe deposit box. TheLetter had everything prepared at her law firm, in the event of her death. Richard had not committed to marriage with her, after all these years. She wanted to be sure that Keon was raised with love and support."

"You know I am going with you. Just try and stop me."

"Beth, he probably thinks that new large home is his, too. Do I have news for him? TheLetter had upgraded maybe three years after Keon was born.

Beth then suggested we go to the cemetery, so that I could say goodbye. She already had a picnic basket and blanket in the car, as well as two parasols. TheLetter was from Louisiana, and there your home going was a celebration. Today, we would honor our friend's home going.

I showered and dressed, and Beth drove to the cemetery. We laid the blanket right by the gravesite. The tombstone was a beautiful gray marble that read: TheLetter Delarue, our loving daughter, sister, and friend. That she was. A very loving friend. I missed her so, and I told her just that. Soon, Beth and I were talking about the times when we went skating, to the club, and how TheLetter had trouble getting rid of a guy.

We opened our parasols. We did the New Orleans cakewalk around the burial site, in tribute to our friend. I could feel the sunshine on my face with its gentle warmth. The thick, cool, green grass pushed up between my toes with every step. My spirit had warmed. It was as if TheLetter was right there with us. Laughing and doing the cake walk. Her sweet and gilded spirit brushed against us, letting us know that she was still close. For those few short moments, it was as before. We were together again. It felt as though she was trying to tell me something. What?

TheLetter starved for that American pie type of life. The kind they sell in soap operas. A wonderful, loving, and devoted husband, with money, a large home, and children. Plenty of children to run her crazy. Kids that she could pour all of her love on, and then pray in her private closet for their safety. We laughed, ate cheese and crackers, and drank wine. We toasted TheLetter. Her heart was pure gold.

"Beth. Do you think she went to heaven?"

"Yes. If anyone deserves to go, it's TheLetter."

"Yeah. But, she didn't deserve what happened to her. I bet she was scared. I wish I had been there to help. Instead, I was arguing with that fool, Albert."

"Carmen, don't go carrying regret for something you had absolutely no control of. It's not your fault. Besides, you can't turn back the hands of time. None of us can."

"I wish I could though. I would change a lot of things. A whole lot of things. What about Keon? She'll never see him grow up, graduate school, or get married."

"He's eight, so I'm sure he knows what's going on, Carmen. Keon, I'm sure he's traumatized. now, he is up there with his so-called father. It's going to take a lot of money to raise three children by yourself, Carmen."

"Oh, no. We'll be fine. TheLetter had a lot of money left from her grandfather's estate. Plus, a million dollar life insurance policy. I'm to sell her home, give the predetermined sums to each family member, and put the rest into Keon's trust. That's why I'm worried. Richard doesn't know about all this money. He probably thinks that he's getting everything, like the house, car, and a moderate policy. I don't even want to think about what he might do, when he finds out. Have the police found any suspects to TheLetter's murder?"

"No, they stopped looking. I've called until I'm blue in the face. They did question your friend, Albert."

"What? Why?"

"Turns out he was at the club that night. According to Crystal, he and TheLetter danced to a few songs, until TheLetter slapped him and left him on the dance floor."

"What did he do?"

"Don't know. Crystal couldn't hear, and TheLetter never said. However, the police questioned and released him. I do know that something is not right with the way she died. But, they haven't found evidence to the contrary. I pulled a few strings and got a copy of the news tape that police took at the scene. Thought you'd like to see it."

"I do want to see it. I'll check it out as soon as we get back."

"You know Carmen, if I die, I want to be buried with all my shoes. I don't want anyone else to get them."

"Beth. If we put all of your shoes in there, then it won't be enough room for you."

"And I'm not through shopping. No, sir. There are shoes still calling my name. Many more stores to conquer."

Now, I knew Beth was drunk. Talking about burying her with her shoes. Besides, she is much too conceited to die.

I watched the tape that night for what seemed like a hundred times. It looked like the regular crowd of nosey people at the scene of a crime. However, something about it was not right. I just could not put my finger on it.

That night I did something that I had not done since high school. I began to write. To write about my emotions and frustrations. The things that made me happy, and what made me sad. My accomplishments and desires. Hopes and dreams. Successes and disappointments.

I began to put my life on paper. My heart and soul poured forth onto paper and I began to cry. It was a cleansing of sorts. A private way to rid the skeletons from my closet, and purge my spirit of the demons that had tormented me for years. Of course, it did not happen overnight. Nevertheless, it was a start.

To fall in love and have the company of a man is something I did not seek on a long-term basis. I had resolved to the life of a single woman. A divorced mother, and darn proud of it. If I spend more than a month dating a man, it was more of a tactical maneuver, then an emotional one. My children were my solace, and the only things that resembled normalcy to me.

So far our lives, Bethany, TheLetter, and mine, were not anything like those we read about in storybooks, or saw on the soap operas our mothers watched. The reality of it all was that it was brutal and painful. As the minutes turned to hours, the days, weeks, months, and years passed like a volatile blur. I grew tired of the repeated promises of love. Unfortunately, there were more sad days than happy ones, at all too much of a sacrifice. Looking back on my past the only thing that brings a smile to my face, and that I did not regret, were my children. I clung to them. They were my fountain of peace.

Dear TheLetter,

    Today was a good day. I began to write again. I'm not saying that I'm healed or anything, however, it is a start. I know that you know we were at your gravesite today. Trying to spread a little cheer where there had been turmoil. Beth says she wants to take her shoes when it's time to meet her maker. He'll probably send her packing on the first cloud, if she shows up with all those possessions. I never would have believed that I would lose you. Who knows. Maybe one day soon my heart will stop aching and I can get a full night's sleep.
    The tune of time marches on and I will never be the same. I miss you girl, and I love you.

Lil Sis,
Carmen

CHAPTER 23

Bethany and I arrived in Minneapolis that following Wednesday morning. It was an unusually cold and brisk day for late July. We immediately hailed a cab, and went to a posh hotel in the heart of downtown Minneapolis. Our suite at the Plaza Hotel was ready and tastefully decorated. Beth had a real appreciation for that. A gift basket from the hotel was on this beautiful round mahogany table in the center of the living room area. I took the room to the left, and Beth took the one to the right. We had brunch in the hotel restaurant, after freshening up.

"I'm nervous, Beth."

"Don't be. Richard doesn't know what's about to happen. He knows he is to bring Keon with him, because he will be part of the proceedings. But, he doesn't know anything else. By the time he realizes what's going on, it will be too late. The police will be there to keep peace, and two officers from the sheriff's department will be there to escort him."

"I know. I still have this bad feeling."

"Well, I'm with you. So, do not worry. If the brother decides to jump bad, one of the officers will take a stick to his ass. Richards' greedy, but he is not stupid. He would not dare do anything. It's noon already. We have just enough time to catch a cab, and get to the bank. That file will need to go to the court officer today. Then we'll come back and rest until tomorrow morning."

That night I could not sleep. Therefore, I sat up and read my copy of TheLetter's file. A liberty I took before delivering it to the court officer earlier today. I began to feel ill and disgusted with the information that unfolded. It was only eight p.m., so, I called the house and asked to speak to Keon. Richard insisted that Keon had already gone to bed, but I could hear crying in the background. My heart sank. I could hardly wait for Thursday morning.

Bethany and I arrived at the attorney's office thirty minutes early, so that we could be in place before Richard arrived. As we exited the elevator and checked in with the receptionist, the staff extended their condolences. They spoke highly of TheLetter's accomplishments and wonderful personality. They further stated that. "Her presence is missed."

The meeting will be at nine a.m. in a large corner conference room. We were in awe of the dramatic setting. There was a huge oval cherry conference table in the center, with a beautiful satinwood inlay design framing the perimeter, surrounded by twelve elegant chairs. The chairs were ornate in nature, and their seats were of a beautiful blue tapestry print reminiscent of an English countryside scene. The table sat on a large blue tapestry rug, which complimented the fabric on the chairs. Underneath the rug were rich cherry wood floors. The walls had books neatly placed in custom built-in bookcases. The decoration of that firm was expensive was, and Beth was absorbing it all. It was a nice respite for me to see her inventorying that room.

As we were escorted to our seats Beth leaned in and whispered, "I must ask who their designer is. Do you know how difficult it is to find antique rugs like this in mint condition?"

The court officer, Mrs. Garcia; and legal representative, Mr. Clark, were seated at the head of the table. The original file that I obtained from TheLetter's safe deposit box was sitting on the table in front of them. Behind them was a glass wall, which gave way to a picturesque view of downtown. It was breath taking.

We had just sat down, when Richard and Keon arrived. When Keon saw me, he immediately broke loose from Richard and ran to my arms. He was hanging on to my neck so tightly, and he was trembling.

"Auntie Carmen, did you come to get me. Please take me home with you. Don't leave me here," Keon whimpered, as he burrowed his face into my chest.

"Keon, get back over here, and quit that whining, like some little punk," Richard said.

One of the officers placed his hand on Richard's shoulder. "Take a seat, sir. The kid can sit with the lady."

Richard slowly took his seat, while fixing his glare on Keon.

"Yes, baby," I whispered to Keon. "You're going home with Auntie Carmen." Keon clung to my arm as he sat in the chair to my left, which was between the court officer and myself. Bethany sat to my right. Richard sat on the opposite side, rapidly tapping his fingers on the table, and breathing so hard and fast that a fog appeared on the table. The court officer stood directly behind him.

The proceedings began and moved swiftly. Richard's shock and disappointment was apparent. His face cracked like glass.

"What the hell do you mean? She gets the money and my son? What kind of crap is this?"

"Mr. Warren, please take your seat. The stipulations of this will are legal and very precise. In exchange for your freedom, you will not contest this," said the legal representative. "You are to remove all of your personal effects from the home, immediately. There are two officers outside waiting to escort you. A locksmith will be present to change all locks. Furthermore, you are not to have any contact with Ms. Robertson, or Keon, unless it is set up in advance, and monitored by a court assigned officer. Do you understand?"

"Hell, naw, I don't understand? I lived with that stupid bitch woman for years. We are common-law married, and that is my child, not Carmen's."

"Mr. Warren, certain facts have been well documented and brought to our attention. The color photos of Ms. DeLarue's face after altercations, copies of police reports, as well as tape recordings and documents of your adverse conversations with her about abortions. In addition, you demanding proof of paternity. You are not a suitable parent for young Keon," she said. "There is enough here to file charges against you. In meeting with the deceased requests, we will not file charges at this time. However, break any of these requirements and you will be arrested. Now, sit down."

"Okay, I'll continue," said the legal representative. Ms. Robertson is the legal guardian of Keon, and his trust fund. She is also the executor of the estate. That includes a 401K totaling five hundred thousand dollars, a life insurance policy for one million, one personal savings account for three hundred thousand, the home, and the car. The home is to be sold and the car, as well. Proceeds from those sales are to be in trust for Keon. Monies maybe deposited or withdrawn at Ms. Robertson's discretion. Checks of five thousand each will be printed and sent by registered mailed to the listed immediate family members, with inclusion of Ms. Childs."

"Ms. Childs, we need you to sign some forms and then that ends this meeting. Our office took the liberty of obtaining a realtor for the sale of the home, and one of our junior associates is interested in buying Ms. DeLarue's BMW at a very reasonable price. I'll have him contact you at the Plaza," said the representative.

"That will be fine, Mr. Clark. Thank you," I said. "Let's go, Keon."

"This ain't over yet, bitch. You'll get yours," muttered Richard.

"Mr. Warren, if you'll go with the officers, they'll escort you to pick up your belongings."

Richard's eyes were fixated on us, as we exited the conference room. He had a cold steel glare that pierced through me. I could not wait to get as far from him as possible. Our flight was to leave for Friday morning.

We returned to the hotel to change for dinner. During that time Mr. Blake, the junior associate, arrived. He was waiting in the lobby, as we exited the elevator. What a gorgeous hunk of man. Extremely polite and precise with his words.

"Good afternoon, Ms. Robertson. I am Keith Blake, I worked with Ms. DeLarue."

"Yes, hello. This is Bethany Childs, and this is Keon, TheLetter's son."

"Hi, Keon. I recognize you from the pictures on your mother's desk. She loved you very much. Ms. Childs, nice to make your acquaintance."

"Same here."

"Ms. Roberston, is something wrong?"

"Uh, no. You just seem familiar to me."

"Well, I assure you we haven't met. I would remember an enchanting woman, such as yourself."

"I guess so."

"As you know I would like to purchase the BMW, Ms. Robertson. It would mean a lot to me to have this vehicle. Ms. DeLarue was well respected and loved at our office, and that car holds special memories. If you agree, I have a cashier's check and the forms for you to sign.

There's a notary present in the hotel, if you'll step this way."

"I'll be right back, Beth."

It took less than five minutes to sign the forms. Mr. Blake seemed passionate about TheLetter. Beth, Keon, and I hailed a cab and headed to Goodfellow's historic restaurant. The décor impeccably done, the food delectable, and the wine list was extensive. A glass of wine will help to soothe me. Keon loved the music and the food, though he did not eat much. As soon as we returned to the hotel, he fell asleep across Beth's bed.

"Well, Carmen it's over. How do you feel?"

"Scared. Did you hear what that fool said, Beth?"

"Yeah, but he's not going to do anything. That man is history. He's just mad that he didn't get TheLetter's money."

"Yeah, maybe. I don't know what it is, but something is really nagging at me. I wish I had that crime scene video tape. Hey, didn't that Mr. Blake look familiar to you?"

"Actually, he did. But, I couldn't put my finger on it. Anyway, Carmen, you have your son Jerrick."

"And?"

"Your son is a great amateur detective. He is actually a bit of a wiz, of all things electronic."

265

"And?"

"My goodness, woman. Call your son, tell him what is going on, get the tape and get this ball rolling."

"Oh, my Lord, Beth. You're a genius. I'll call him, now."

"Well, while you're doing that, I'll check on Keon. He really should go ahead and take a bath, then get dressed for bed. Poor kid is exhausted and he seems so rattled all the time."

I ran to my room to get my purse and called Jerrick, and the attorney. It was not thirty minutes before the attorney called me to inform me that they sent the video to Atlanta to Jerrick's attention as I requested by courier. I immediately breathed a sigh of relief, and wrote a quick email to Jerrick explaining what I wanted him to do with the video once it arrived. Suddenly, there was a loud knock on the door, which broke my rhythm as I typed the email on the laptop.

"Beth, did you order anything?"

"No. Did you get the video?"

"Yes, they are sending it today by courier to Atlanta. I was just sending Jerrick an email detailing what I want him to do. I'll get the door." As I approached the door, it struck me that there was not a peephole in this hotel door. Upon opening the door, it crossed my mind that I really should have asked who it was, but it was too late. When I opened the door, Richard rushed in.

"Excuse you. I didn't invite you in. What are you doing here, anyway?"

"Look, Carmen. TheLetter wanted you to raise our son, so, I can kind of understand that. But, it's not fair that after all of our years together, that I don't get anything."

"Oh, I think it's fair. She made the money."

"Come on. I'm willing to make a deal with you. Give me just five hundred thousand and we'll call it a wash. I won't bother you or Keon anymore."

"You piece of shit. You're willing to put a price on your son. You make me sick. Get your ass out of here before I call the police. You heard the requirements. You're not supposed to be here."

"Look, here bitch. I could take you to court and force you to give Keon up. A big time Atlanta doctor like yourself, wouldn't want that pearl image of yours messed up."

"What are you talking about, Richard?"

"Ah-h, don't play innocent with me. I know all about you and your dead friend Saree. TheLetter told me everything. What do you think your yuppie circle and the court's will think about that?"

"I think you have your facts mixed up. You don't know what you're talking about. I, also, know that TheLetter let you stay around for the benefit of your son. She knew you were still involved with a lover. Yeah, that's right. Didn't think we knew about that, did you. Now, get the hell out of here."

"What is this? What are you doing, Carmen?" I had forgotten about the email I had written Jerrick regarding the video of the crime scene. The laptop was open, sitting in Richard's line of sight on the desk. Richard could see every word I had written. "You stupid bitch. See, I was trying to be nice to your ass." He pulled a gun from his pocket. "Get over here and start writing your goodbye letter. I'll just have to get that money and my son back the hard way."

"I am not writing a letter. You're just going to have to shoot me."

"Think you're brave, huh?" Richard raised his hand and hit me across my face. He held up two fingers and sternly said, "You got one more time to mess with me." Grabbing me by my arm, and yanking me across the room. "Type the damn letter."

"Lucky you have that gun, or I'd kick your ass. You slug."

Suddenly, a strong knock came at the door. "Police, is everything okay?"

"No," I yelled.

The police rushed in, with the hotel manager and hotel security. Richard was immediately handcuffed, and taken into custody without further incident. Thank God Beth was listening at the door, and called the police.

"I'll get you for this," he repeatedly yelled, as they took him away."

"Ms. Robertson, we'll be back in a few minutes for a statement," said one of the officers. I nodded in agreement.

"Are you all right, Carmen?"

"Yes, Beth. I'll be okay. Thanks for calling the police."

My mind was swimming, as I sat down at the writer's desk. Looking at the screen, I could not imagine why Richard went berserk.

"Oh, my God, Beth, that Richard is crazier than we could have ever imagined."

"Yes he is," Beth uttered in a shallow voice. "But, I have something more important I need you to see, C.C. I discovered it while assisting Keon with his bath."

"What, Beth?"

"Just follow me. And maintain yourself. Don't scare him."

I followed Beth to the bathroom. Little Keon was playing in the bubbles. Beth pointed to his back. My heart was suddenly overwhelmed with anger and sadness at the same time. Covering my mouth to hold in the grunt. I knelt down by the side of the tub, and picked up the washcloth.

"Hey, Keon. Having fun?"

"Yes, Auntie Carmen."

"Well, let me help you wash your back?"

"Okay."

"Beth, why don't you go down to the gift shop and get one of those disposable cameras. I want to take pictures of my nephew," I said as calmly as possible, fighting back the tears. That so and so is going to rot in jail for abuse and murder, if it's the last thing I do.

LOVE & LIFE

L ying and

O bstructive

V iolating

E motions

L achrymose

I nfidelity

F allacy

E bony

L iving

O bliterate

V engence

E dge

CHAPTER 24

I returned to Atlanta, after another week. Keon had no trouble fitting in. He had already known my kids from previous encounters, and my son loved having a little brother.

They had not missed any school, I got Keon registered, and I promised to take them shopping the following weekend. Which was fine with them. I returned to the office, and dove into work. There were regular reflections of Saree' and TheLetter, and many sleepless nights. The only activities I went to were school events and church. I relaxed, curled up with a good book, my dog Nemesis, and a glass of wine. From my favorite chaise lounge, I passed many hours.

My emotions churned like a roller coaster. Some days were better than other days; but I would often spend hours staring out a window, or just into space. Jerrick's amateur sleuthing of the video turned up some questions and awful details that had been overlooked by the police. They have agreed to reopen TheLetter's case. That is a wonderful break for us all. I thanked God for answering prayers. Yes, Richard was in jail awaiting trial on the abuse charges, and TheLetter's case reopened!

In 1991, my younger brother, Kennard, was murdered. All for greed, and the love of drugs. That threw me for another loop, and devastated my son. I just was not sure how much more I could take before I broke. A wall was building up around me, and it had no windows or doors. It is said that, "The Lord knows how much you can bear." I was beginning to think that He was losing count of my load. I adored Kennard! The fact that someone could take his life, for a few dollars, without even blinking, was frightening.

Well, at least, I did not have to think about Richard. He was to face charges of assault, and carrying a weapon without a permit. TheLetter's law firm was very helpful, and agreed to keep me posted on the events. I did not have to attend any of the proceedings. Once they have finished with him, San Antonio's finest would like to interrogate him, as well as, Mr. Blake.

It was an unseasonably cool evening in September. Bible study night in the church's main sanctuary. I was starting to become a zombie. Sleep escaped me. Just going through the motions of life. Not caring whether I had a date or not. Not wanting to foster a new relationship with anyone. Why let someone get too close?

"Hi, Carmen. Good to see you tonight," A familiar voice said.

"Hi, Leon. Good to see you, too. Though, I haven't been seeing you."

"Well, this is a large sanctuary. I usually sit on the left side. Figured I'd change up a bit. And looks like it was for the better."

"Yeah, well. Enjoy the services."

"Wait, Carmen. Why don't you and the children sit here with me?"

"No, thank you. I'd rather not."

"We can go for a bite to eat and some ice cream afterwards."

"I said, no. But, thanks for the offer."

I knew he was disappointed, but I really did not care. He had too many strikes against him. I did not want to get close to anyone, and he was a man, a man, a man. Leon continued his campaign of trying to get close to me. He even tried to get in good with my children by bringing them goodies to services. Though I declined to give him my phone number, and turned him down repeatedly for dates, he was relentless in his quest. I began to come late and leave early, so that he would not have an opportunity to speak with me. I even considered not going to church anymore to avoid this man. One evening as I was entering the church vestibule, there he was standing at the door, like a guard.

"Good evening, Ms. Robertson. How are you?"

"Fine, Leon. How are you?"

"Great, but I'd be better if you'd agree to go out with me?"

"I don't date. I just don't have the time."

"So, what do you do? Work all the time, and come to church?"

"That's my business Mr. Johnson. Now, if you'll excuse me."

"Carmen, wait. I don't want to be a pest. Really, I don't. But, woman I got it bad for you. Let me make you an offer. Give me one chance. One opportunity to change your heart. If you still don't want to continue seeing me after one date, then I promise to leave you alone."

That got my attention. One date with this joker is all I have to invest in him. Then I can get rid of him. "Okay. One date then you will leave me alone. No ifs, ands, or buts. Next Friday evening. Meet me at the Shark Bar at eight p.m."

"Great. You won't be sorry Ms. Robertson."

"Yeah, right. Tell it to someone that cares."

The week was passing quicker than I would like. I found myself strangely intrigued, and anticipating the evening. I have known of this young man since my high school days. Yet, there had been no real interaction in years. An investigation needed to be completed. I made some phone calls to mutual friends to do a *Down Home* background check. Everyone spoke highly of him. However, there is always something.

At this stage, my children were old enough to stay at home alone, and Keon was well mannered but seemed to be nervous all the time. I guess his adjustment is not going to be as easy as I had hoped. I alerted my neighbor, who was a widower, a mother, and a good friend, to keep an eye on the kids for a few hours. The children were shocked and thrilled that I was going out. I drove to the restaurant after services. I was so nervous and annoyed at the same time. Here I was wasting my time to meet a man for dinner. I already knew how it was going to turn out.

I parked my car and tried to balance myself on my high heels, as I maneuvered from the lot to the front door. There was a nice sized crowd out that evening, and the air was thick with humidity. Thank Goodness someone turned on the air conditioner and ceiling fans. I took a seat at the bar, and ordered a margarita on the rocks. The lighting was prefect. Beautifully placed chandeliers hung from the ceiling, and each table had a crisp white tablecloth, and a candle.

A middle-aged couple that caught my eye. Their table had balloons hovering from it, with confetti thrown about. Obviously, celebrating some milestone in their lives. They appeared to be so happy. Laughing, whispering to each other, and touching. Maybe a true and lasting love does exist.

Well, well, this man was late. So, I thought. Someone then tapped me on the shoulder.

"Hi, Carmen."

"Hi, Leon."

"I have a table for us. Would you like to join me?"

"Sure."

"Have her drink brought to the table bartender. Thank you."

I liked that. He tipped the bartender and then ever so gently placed his hand on my waist, as he escorted me to our table. Which had a bouquet of a dozen red roses waiting for me. He also pulled out my chair. Well, that will be a few points for his good manners. There I was thinking this man was on C. P. Time, when in fact, he was early. A fine quality to have, but I had better not get my hopes up. Anyway, what does it matter? I am just here to get him off my back. To shut him up.

"You look beautiful tonight, Carmen."

"Thank you."

"Hmm. Thank you for the opportunity. Let me say that I know you've been hurt before. But, I'm not going to even try to pretend that I know how you feel, or what has happened to you. All I can say is that I am a man. A responsible and loving man. If you will allow me, I will restore your belief in men. In time you'll share with me, when you feel ready."

"Wow. That was a mouthful."

We continued our conversation. The man was true to his word. I did not regret the date. I was pleasantly surprised. This man was a total Gentleman, had goals, manners, and intelligence. Turned out he was a good dancer, too. *Truth Be Told*, I was enjoying myself. However, I am not sure I would outwardly admit it. I never knew Leon was this deep.

This six foot two smooth chocolate man with broad shoulders, long legs, and a bright smile, was attempting to melt my heart. However, he cannot claim a victory just yet. When dating people always put their best foot forward. Somehow, along the path things had ended tangled up. The time for false facades slowly melts away, and the true person breaks through. Just give him time and he will crumble like a sand castle. In fact, give any man enough time and rope, and he will hang himself.

I decided not to get my hopes up. Each heartbreak or disappointment was like a virus infecting my body and devouring the fresh red pieces of my heart and soul. Leaving behind the tattered flesh to decay. I hate men. They are so stupid. Why is it we cannot be more considerate and caring of the other, and aware of the pain our actions can inflict? Why do we not exhibit the exuberance of past queens, kings, princes, and princesses? A person may speak "I love you" all day long, but their actions reflect disrespect.

I do not trust a man further than I could throw him. He could be Mr. Right today, and Mr. Hyde tomorrow.

"Ms. Robertson. Are you having a good time?"

"Yes. It's been an okay evening."

"Um-hm. A woman like you. I know your mind has been ticking away this whole evening."

"Well, I...."

"Please. Let me say this. I am not some immature boy that doesn't know how to love a woman. You see, I want a second date with you. So, I'm going to share something with you. I know a woman won't respect a man that doesn't take responsibility, or isn't industrious. If she doesn't respect you, she'll rule you. If she rules you, you're more like her child than her man. Carmen, you don't have to worry about ruling me, because I am a responsible man. Therefore, you will easily respect me and together we can achieve unspeakable measures. Now, with that said, I'll lighten up."

"You're well spoken, Leon. However, they are just words. Words I've heard in church. However, the proof is in the pudding. I hear you talking the talk, but can you walk the walk?"

"Oh, yes my dear, I can. And I'll tear that wall you have down, too. One beautiful brick at a time. What you don't know is that you are a beautiful diamond in the rough, just waiting to come gleaming through. It takes a long time to unmask a beautiful jewel. Cheers."

This night ended on an intriguing note. Leon walked me to my car, and I gave him my phone number. Let the games begin. I could not resist contemplating the possibilities as I drove home. I really needed to get a grip on my reality. There are no fairytale relationships or marriages. The number of truly happy couples are far and few between. People seem to have difficulty being above board and honest with each other from the onset. Usually, because they fear losing that person. However, that is the best time to be your true self, at the beginning. You do not waste an individual's time, and you save them heartbreak. However, there are those that still lay in false hopes of changing a person, even knowing they are not compatible with them.

I NEVER DREAM

I never knew with whom all my dreams
would come true,
Now I know because God blessed me with
you.

Someone to share all the seasons in time
someone who would only be mine,
Now I know that all the while
for whom I was waiting – when I saw your
smile.

You have changed my life with the warmth
Of your love, and with you I feel safe
This is the beginning of all we will share
To you I want to give myself.
Two separate people, joined by one beautiful
love.

Carmen

CHAPTER 25

Time marched on. Leon and I continued to date. He was not overbearing. Weeks had passed without a single annoyance. We did not spend hours on the phone listening to the other breathe. Every conversation was of reasonable length and informative.

I told him of my hopes and dreams, of plans for the future. I wanted to be a top rate doctor, with a successful practice. I also wanted to own some businesses. Such as an assisted living facility, and a restaurant. I believed that people should save their money and plan for their future retirement. Children should be educated, and each generation should be more successful. I also wanted to travel and see the world. To experience new people, places, cultures, and foods. I like time to myself to do whatever I wanted to do. Mostly, to read.

Leon concurred with my thoughts. He liked to read, as well. He also owned his own business, traveled, and learned about new cultures. Leon believed in saving, and did have sufficient funds in the bank right now, especially after the death of his wife. He wanted to go back to finish college. Currently, he contracted his maintenance company services for a local shopping mall, but wanted to contract with more businesses in the city. He has ten, now.

There was always something to learn from this intelligent brother. Yet, I still laid in wait for him to make a mistake- like a lioness behind the tall grass of the Serengeti, waiting for her prey. One slip and she would devour it. I was always brutally honest with him about my thoughts and beliefs. Nevertheless, he took it like a Champ.

We dated one to two times a week. He even made time for my children by planning outings that included them. From walks in the park, football games, movies, the circus, and even fishing. My favorite was home videos and popcorn. He even attended my boy's football games, and my daughter's volleyball games. However, I still did not fully trust him, and challenged him at every turn. I was insistent on keeping him at arm's length. Over the years' man had become my adversary, not my ally.

Leon had been a widower for five years and the father of two adult sons. Both sons resided in California. This is where they grew up and were educated. Their maternal grandparents were there as well as several uncles and aunts. He had hopes for a long and happy marriage until she died. They had married young and he was happy for the years they had together. He moved to Atlanta because there were too many memories that kept him with one foot in the past and he knew he needed to forge a new life and California would not allow for that.

I was reclining on my chaise lounge one Saturday morning as I contemplated these aspects of the past weeks, when the call came.

"Hello."

"Hi C.C. What's going on girlfriend?"

"Nothing. What's going on with you, Beth?"

"Oh, a little this and a little that. Okay, enough with the Chit-Chat. How's it going with your new man?"

"He's not my man. Thank you very much. We're just dating."

"Oh, I see. But, this could lead to something more, right?"

"Well, I haven't thought about that yet. We're still trying to get to know each other."

"Does that mean you haven't slept together?"

"First of all, I sleep every night here in my own bed. Alone. Secondly, why does it always have to be about sex? If couples slept together all the time without the benefit of marriage, then you leave nothing to work towards. Besides, I have enough Ghosts arms hanging onto my soul as it is."

"You're right. There's no rush. So, you think of yourselves as a couple. Huh?"

"Oh, Beth. What am I going to do with you?"

"How about keep loving me, and know that I will not leave you alone about men?"

"Hold on Carmen. Chad wants to speak with you."

"Hi, Carmen. This is Chad. I know I don't usually get in the middle of you and Beth's girl talk, but I just wanted to give a different point of view. May I?"

"I guess so."

"You've known me for as long as I've been married to your girl, right?"

"Right."

"I love Beth, our children, and our life together. There's nothing I would do to mess that up. Have I ever done anything to cause you to think that I'm not an honorable man?"

"No. Actually, there are no real complaints about you from Beth. Except, sometimes we do poke fun at the manner in which you do things. You know loving those tools and thinking you're Mr. Fixit."

"Oh, yeah? Well, I'm going to have to speak with her about that. My point here is that not every man is a sorry sack of bones. I know you've been hurt in the past, baby. If I could, I would strangle ever one of those jokers for you. They didn't know what they had, Carmen. Therefore, they didn't appreciate it. This guy sounds like he's for real. All I'm saying is give him a chance. Don't build that wall so high that you'll miss out on an opportunity for true happiness. Sometimes you have to go through a whole barrel to reach that special jewel. Okay, I love you, and here's Beth."

"I love you, too. And I'll talk to you later, Carmen. Goodbye."

"All right, Beth. Goodbye."

It struck me as strange when Chad intervened in our conversation. He certainly made an impression upon me. He is a great man. One of the few in existence. If he was putting stock behind Leon, then maybe I should reconsider my position. Why is destruction so easy; and, recovery is hard? Nevertheless, I was beginning to feel as though I wanted to make that journey.

I allowed Leon to come over and spend Saturday with the kids and I. We started the day with breakfast. He played touch football with my sons and spent quality time with my daughter discussing her interests.

"Can I help you with that, Carmen?"

"Thanks, Leon. But, I am used to doing my own hair. At least, when I don't get to the shop."

"Maybe. But, why wash it yourself when you don't have to?"

"Well, okay."

My goodness. It felt so wonderful. Leon was a master with massaging my scalp as he washed. I had never had a man to wash my hair. It was so relaxing, and revealing. Then suddenly I wondered what he really wanted. Leon was not a formerly educated man.

He was an owner of a maintenance company. He seems to be doing very well. However, I do not know for sure. He could have a lot of debt. Leon rents a two-bedroom condominium, and drives an older model car. A car that he keeps very clean, and in good working condition. I wondered if he still supported his sons. I could not respect a man that did not take care of his children. He can do nothing for me. They are the flesh of his flesh, and blood of his blood. I believed that a man should love his children more than a new woman in his life. Their well-being should be of utmost importance to him. However, they are grown and mostly independent now.

This man touched my soul. He oiled my scalp, and brushed my hair. I could not help laying my head on his knee as he gently stroked my hair with my brush.

"Leon, can I ask a rather personal question?"

"You can ask me anything."

"Do you support your sons financially?"

"Yes, I help them when needed. Using the life insurance benefits from their mother's policy. I send a regular living stipend each month to assist them. California is an inexpensive place to live and they have their heads on straight. I do not get to see them as often as I would like because of our schedules. But I promised their mother I would always take care of them no matter how old and grown they got to be…"

"Do you ever skip paying a bill to buy something else that you want?"

"No. What made you ask that?"

"I feel it is deplorable for a man to have children that he doesn't support both financially and emotionally. If you were like that, then I wouldn't want anything to do with you."

"So, it's like that, Carmen."

"Yes, just like that."

"Well, I admire you for caring. No other sister has ever asked me that. I do drive out to see them every year and spend about a month with them and they fly here from time to time as well."

"Who knows? Maybe that can change."

This man was feeding me. This man was a complete person. This man will have my heart. Leon prepared a simple dinner for us, and cleaned the kitchen. The brownie points were mounting.

The children had gotten sleepy and gone up to bed. Leon and I continued to watch our movie. The one about a woman who was supposed to meet her love on top of the Empire State Building on Valentine's Day. However, she did not because of an accident. He later found out why. It was such a moving story.

I became amorous and leaned into Leon's side, as he put his arms around me. We looked deep into each others eyes and began to kiss. It had been so long, I almost forgot how. His touch was soft and gentle. His body smelled of a seductive cologne. My loins cried out for this man.

"Why don't we go upstairs, Leon?"

"Are you sure?"

"Yes!"

I took his big strong hand, and led him up to my bedroom. A place that he had not been before. I dimmed the lights and clicked on some smooth jazz. It was a romantic setting, and I was ready. We continued our kissing, hugging, and caressing. His muscularly sculpted body felt wonderful next to me. When he removed his shirt, I thought I was going to faint. Things changed as the moment deepened.

"Carmen. What's wrong?"

"Nothing. What makes you think something is wrong?"

"Because you have your eyes closed, and your body has tensed up. Are you scared?"

"Well, yes. A little bit. I'm sorry, Leon. I thought I was ready. I was okay until we both shed our clothes."

"Baby, never be sorry about how you feel. We shouldn't be doing this anyway. I guess we both got weak. Get dressed and let's go for a bite to eat. This can wait. Wait until you're ready. Whenever that is. Wait until you can look at me without fear. Wait until we're married."

"Slow your roll, man. I'm not thinking about marriage right now. I don't know you that well, yet. Let's just play this by ear."

I was trying to be up front. Right then, that very moment, I knew that he was the jewel and that I could love him. This man's points went off the charts. I wondered if all the past disappointments, and heartaches were to prepare me for this moment. I had thanked God for the roses in my life, but never for the thorns. I did not see Leon's dark skin, his occupation, salary, standard of car, or any of those other socially accepted guidelines that most women use to gauge what a good man is. I saw his soul and his golden heart.

In time I will totally heal, and be able to give of myself without reservation or suspicion. I was sure that if I was going to make it, Leon is the man that I would be able to make it. We had similar aspirations and goals, and he had plenty of patience. Who knows, maybe we will end up married. Life is a journey with many roads and turns. The one you choose determines your fate. It can be blissfully happy, or sad with a lot of turmoil. However, each path is a learning experience. Take that knowledge and make your life better, and wiser.

__AUTUMN__

Autumn is my favorite time of year.
The colors so bold and clear.
Red, orange, yellow, green and gold
are so vivid in my eyes stream.

Mesmerized as the leaves dance gently with
God's wind
A daydream centers of loving and wonderful
times
Why isn't life as beautiful as Autumn?

Relationships in the spring of my life
were quite turbulent.
Yet, I endured them through the
summers heat.

When the heat was in it's cooling
off stage.
I was blessed with this relationship
in the fall, and I'm sure he'll
be with me until the end of winter.
Carmen

AFTERWARD

Women have certain strongholds in life. Whether we readily admit them or not. Throughout history, women have been particular about both. It may be in unadulterated excess, simply magic, or some type of swinging appeal. Regardless, we must have our shoes and our men, and even our clothes. It makes me wonder why we have a shoe fetish and what is the correlation to men?

From an item of practical purpose, shoes have propelled to reflect our passions, ideals, culture, prospective, weaknesses, and our strengths. We either hide them, if they are an embarrassment; or flaunt them, if we think they are the stuff.

Do we reflect in our soles, who we pick to be our soul mates? From the black boots of the queen Victorian era to our stiletto heels. Watch out now! Relationships are relative. It is all in how we relate to one another. How we communicate and react. This depends on our backgrounds, beliefs, values, and morals. We could each see the same thing differently.

About Sharon Bennett & Beatrice Moore

Sharon Bennett (right) is a health care professional. She has a Bachelors of Arts, and a bachelor's of science degree. She currently resides in the Atlanta, GA area near her adult children & her grandchildren. Shoe Fetish is her third published work, revised in 2015. It is a 3-book series. Her poem entitled "I Never Dreamed." It was published in True Reflections, and won The Library of Poetry's Editor's Choice award. She had articles placed in several business publications. Sharon's second work, authored independently, was THE L.E. BENNETT STORY: Living the Dream, a biography about her father's civil rights activities, and the ministry. Life raised in the church had its moments.

Beatrice Moore (left) has earned both a bachelor and master's degree and works as an independent educational consultant, specializing in the area of mathematics. She has co-authored numerous mathematics textbooks and published professional articles in various education publications. She has realized a lifelong dream of authoring fiction with the publication of Shoe Fetish. She resides in the Houston, TX, metro area with her family. Shoe Fetish: A Woman's Love actually was an Amazon top seller in its first release. The authors have been friends since 6th grade and Shoe Fetish 2: Grown Into High Heels is the sequel.

BOOK CLUB QUESTIONS FOR DISCUSSION

1. How do you feel about Carmen's revelation of God's power and man's resemblance of power?

2. How much of an impact on the girls lives do you feel their parents actually had?

3. Were Carmen's parents right to schedule the abortion, and not pursue legal action?

4. Why did Tony not call Beth after the campus incident? This may be viewed as an opportunity to make lemonade from the lemons life has handed you.

5. Have you been in lemons to lemonade relationships?

6. Were Carmen's emotions for Saree confused?

7. What was another way that Saree could have handled her internal conflicts?

8. Do you have friends similar to the characters presented in this book?

9. What are your thoughts on TheLetter's lifestyle, and her brutal death?

10. How can Carmen get through her objection of men? Will she ever be truly happy?

11. Why was Janette putting up with an abusive relationship?

12. Can a relationship of people from two different social and financial stations really work?

13. The characters evolve from puberty to adulthood and explore sexuality at every junction. How does their journey mirror yours? How is their journey different?

14. The subject of what is now termed as date rape is explored, what are your

thoughts on this subject and what do you feel is the best remedy?

15. What is your Fetish?

PERSONAL NOTES/THOUGHTS